This Is My Surfboard

by

The Sandman (*see profile)

with drawings by
Michael Bell

ABC
BOOKS

A long composition with a Reference
Section that looks at aspects of The
Sandman's life between three years and
15 years of age

Published by ABC Books for the
AUSTRALIAN BROADCASTING CORPORATION
GPO Box 9994 Sydney NSW 2001

Copyright © text, The Sandman, 1996
Copyright © illustration, Michael Bell, 1996

First published August 1996
Reprinted December 1996
Reprinted March 1998
Reprinted September 1999

National Library of Australia
Cataloguing-in-Publication entry
The Sandman 1956– .
 This is my surfboard.

ISBN 0 7333 0534 2.

1. Australian wit and humour – 20th century. I. Australian
Broadcasting Corporation. II. Triple J (Radio station).
III. Title.

A824.3

Illustrated by Michael Bell
Designed by Paul Stanish
Set in 10/¹/₂/12¹/₂pt Koblenz by
Midland Typesetters, Maryborough, Victoria
Printed and bound in Australia by
Australian Print Group, Maryborough, Victoria

5 4

Contents

Author's Note

I would like to thank the following: Angela Moore, Mikey Robins, Helen Razor, Mark Kennedy, Glenn Butcher for the music scores, Paul Livingston, Criena Gerke, the friendly people at Triple J and in particular Michael Bell for his expert drawings.

This Is My Surfboard should be read aloud in a dull monotone voice. Each page is approximately three hundred words. If the page takes you around two minutes ten/ twenty seconds to read then you are more or less in character.

I suggest you read the story first then deal with the Reference Section later. Every time you see an asterisk * after a word, it means you should refer to the footnote at the bottom of the page. Every time you see a number[2], that means there are more thoughts on this subject in the Reference Section.

Any resemblance to anything living or dead between these covers is purely coincidental. In fact I'm coincidental.

I choose to start the story now.

Sandman Character Profile

You'll get more pleasure reading *This Is My Surfboard* if you have a mental picture of me that is consistent, rich in detail, more or less truthful and up to date. Keep in mind I can't always be trusted.

My first name is The. My second name is Sandman. I call myself The Sandman because it adds mystery to an otherwise flat life. Sometimes people call me 'Sandy' and I like that because it sounds warm and loving. I once had a nickname, 'Bandicoot', but it didn't stick.

What do I look like? Since I'm best known as a disembodied voice on the radio, people usually have their own impressions of what I look like. Most seem to think I'm very tall, with blond hair, and that I always have pens in my top pocket. Therefore most people are quite disappointed when they meet me. They make a sound like a double fault, but I'm used to it. For the record, I'm about average height, dark curly hair, swarthy skin, a large nose that bends to the left (that's why I was called Bandicoot, I guess) and liver rings under my eyes. When people meet me they often think I have kidney trouble. I have brown eyes, thick eyebrows, a hairy chest, but not a hairy back. I've got a hairy section at the base of my spine. If my bottom was a doorway then my hairy patch would be a little welcome mat.[1]

I have a fear of success, failure and rejection, so no matter what people think of me I'm never happy. I have a fear of bubbly shop assistants, and a fear of doing a poo in someone else's toilet. I'll drive miles to use my own toilet. You could say that my bathroom is one of my best friends.[2] My second best friend is Nils, who used to live down the road from me when I was growing up. Nils had overprotective parents,[3,4] so it was hard for us to see enough of each other to bond properly.

Relationships wise, I've had one long-term relationship–a blissful six weeks by the sea with Virginia Fleming[5,6] and two flings–an older woman called Gail* at a TAFE college, and Nicole,** who worked in a bric-a-brac shop and wore a burgundy work dress.

I've had a few jobs: a labourer at a brick refractory, wrapping steel coils for export at BHP,[7] a mascot for a car yard,*** using a steam hose at a cake factory, a brief stint selling aluminium, and doing property management for a small real estate firm.[8] I played Rugby League as a reserve,**** was an uncompetitive swimmer, a slow opening bowler and I follow the North Sydney Rugby League team.[9]

I have a pet dog, a cattle/kelpie called The Tight Piece of Work.***** I did have a Persian cat called Jackson (his breath was so bad it stained the wall where his rug was) and I also had a budgie called Peter,****** but the former got arthritis and was put to sleep and the latter, Peter, flew into a cup of hot tea and his legs withered off. Overall, I'd say my favourite animal is the magpie,[10] but I also like greyhounds because when you take them to the beach they can actually catch the seagulls. I don't like puppies though; I don't like anything with a future.

I feel most relaxed near clear, shallow water and I also love sandbars, plus the sound of inboard motor boats.[11] I love watching TV. I don't like wine and I don't like chatting over

---

* *Sandman's Advice to the Unpopular*, page 35
** *Sandman's Advice to the Unpopular*, page 79
*** *Sandman's Advice to the Unpopular*, page 9
**** *Sandman's Advice to the Unpopular*, page 85
***** *Sandman's Advice to the Unpopular*, page 29
****** *Sandman's Advice to the Unpopular*, page 127

dinner. My favourite food is sauce and for dessert I like ice cream with strawberry topping or warm custard with banana and coconut.

My favourite books are *What Bird Is That?* by Neville Cayley, *Inside League* by Roy Masters, *The Horse's Mouth* by Joyce Carey and *In the Firing Line* by the exciting new Tasmanian author David Boon.

I drive a blue Gemini SL automatic[12] with blond corduroy upholstery. It's the perfect car for an insignificant person. Every time you go to overtake something you realise you haven't got enough power, so you go back to where you started from.

I can't stand anyone touching my belly button and I think I look better when my hair is a bit longer.

Chapter 1

Every night after my father had reheated and eaten his dinner–shepherd's pie, steak and onion gravy, silverside with white sauce, or a steak sandwich lightly toasted–he'd come to my room and tell me a story. He'd kneel down beside my bed (I still can hear those cartilages wrestling), clear his throat, wipe his lips with a wrinkled hanky and begin. At first he would sound quite formal as if reading a school composition, but if I seemed interested he'd loosen up. I'm the same: I always blossom when I know people like me.

My father's stories were either set at the beach, or they featured people from the beach. When I was very young he'd simply relocate the classic fairy stories like *Hansel and Gretel* to the coast, replacing the witch's chocolate house with a kiosk made from hot chips, and so on. I remember the image of a kiosk made from hot chips made us both very hungry and we had to suck peppermints to employ the excess saliva that was created.

Later he mixed fantasy with reality to good effect in what you could best describe as 'legendary surf club tales'. Some of them really stick in my mind too. Filthy Phil the senior boat captain who grabbed a horse by the tail then swung it around his head, and the bronze whaler that swam through a patient's legs in an R and R race and attacked the guy wearing the surf belt are two tales that come to mind. I recall the latter one vividly because he described the man in the surf belt as 'a little silky terrier stuck on a leash being attacked by a pig dog'.

Sometimes his stories were funny and he'd laugh as he

1

Hansel and Gretel
(as told by my father)

recalled a particular person or place. My father often laughed at his own jokes and dabbed his watery eyes with the wrinkled hanky. Sometimes he'd do an unexpected fart when he laughed. When someone unexpectedly farts I always find it funny. You not only have the sound of the fart to laugh at, but the person's surprised facial expression as well. You could say that his bedtime stories stuck to me like pilot fish. Once they're attached they're very hard to shake off. I guess that's what makes a pilot fish a good one–an ability to stick to its host.*

So at eight years old, on the strength of those stories, I joined the surf club. Naturally, I expected much from it too. However, I was disappointed when I didn't see a legendary guy called

---

*The pilot fish is a less confident fish that attaches itself to a larger, more important fish for personal gain, like the National Party of Australia.

Bobby with a barrel chest, high insteps that made him walk like a Spanish dancing horse, who could swim three miles with a 44 gallon drum attached to his neck. Or Noel the sinewy beach sprinter who once lifted an impossibly heavy steel girder off a mate to save his life. There was a Noel and a Bobby, but they didn't match the mental pictures I'd formed from listening to the stories. It's like being brought up watching *Thomas the Tank Engine*. When you see your first real train and it doesn't have a face, you feel ripped off.

Despite this initial disappointment I did enjoy the surf club for a while. Being a nipper was fun. We were like startled brumbies running in a pack to somewhere and back every time we heard a whistle, or saw a man with a paunch wave a bright flag. Even though our aim was to please, be it parents, other nippers, or the man with a paunch, we weren't really that competitive. I just followed the most confident boy and did what he did. Success wasn't important. When you're small, you lose concentration too easily to win something twice in a row. For example, one Sunday I'd won the junior wade race and I was waiting to start the beach sprint when I saw a man unloading dirt from the back of a truck. Next thing I know the race had started, but I was still in the marshalling area mesmerised by the man operating the back hoe. At the zoo, recently, I even caught myself watching two workers fix a pothole with some loam while all around me there were hundreds of endangered species with sad faces. Perhaps concentrating on the unimportant stops you from dealing with the important things in life. Perhaps that's why I'm persistent at the things that don't matter.

As I got older I realised that being a success was an important part of being remembered. I also discovered training was an important part of being a success but unless I'm instantly good at something I have no enthusiasm for it and that makes training very difficult.

3

I dabbled briefly with competitive swimming to enhance my surf club performances, but I never won anything, so I was never committed and I was never remembered. I was fine at the start of a season when there were no races, but as it got hotter and the pool filled with recreational swimmers and the races started, I found it hard to concentrate. The solitariness of swimming, the post-exercise hungry feeling, the endless parade of women wearing wet Speedos covered in mobile air bubbles and the lack of success all combined to act like an anchor.[13]

Certain parents drove their children quite hard. (I'm happy to say mine didn't do that.) One boy, David, was made to walk on his tippy toes before every race, so his calf muscles had this lovely almond shape. I guess watching his calf muscles go up and down like tiny elevators was meant to intimidate the other competitors. It's the same principle Willie wagtails* use to intimidate potential intruders.[14] Mind you, David always beat me easily, so maybe there was something in it. Then again, David wasn't liked. Losers are never hated like winners. Losers may be forgotten, but they're never hated.

---

* The Willie wagtail is a small black bird with a long tail that is frequently fanned. The wagtail is common in most parts of Australia. A very active and excitable bird. See What Bird Is That? by Neville Cayley.

Chapter 2

During the early part of Year 8 a desire to be cooler began to grow in me. Consequently, my attention turned away from sport and on to a pursuit of social success. Like anything in life, social success requires hard work too. So in a paddock across the road from our school I started training at being the same as the people I wanted to impress.

Mr Gumley usually drove his son Kerry and me to school and because he didn't like to get caught in the congestion at the gates he'd drop us a block away, so we had to walk across the paddock to get to the actual school grounds. The moment I hit that paddock, which was very private (due to a line of well-established gum trees around the perimeter), I'd start my training. I'd pull my shirt out, tug at my fringe,[15] swear, act morose, spit after every sentence, pull my pants up high or push them extremely low.* For a year I practised at being untidy and rude without getting chastised or ridiculed. That paddock was two and half minutes of paradise in between my parents and the restrictions of school life.

At first I was frightened by this development in me and I resisted it. I even tried to hide it by using my old traits as camouflage. Towards the end of the year though, I realised Kerry had seen everything I did in that paddock anyway and it was only a matter of time before others did too. I often forgot Kerry walking several metres behind. I must have looked quite odd at times, running in tight circles, trying to look at my shadow, arching my body backwards in a series

---

* *Sandman's Advice to the Unpopular*, page 52

of crisp snapping movements. I was confident he wouldn't say anything though. When I cut through his backyard on the way to my place one day I saw Kerry and his next-door neighbour Sofia both naked in his garage and she was urinating in front of him while he watched. She was doing it with such ferocity it was making dust on the garage floor rise up and form a cloud around her ankles. Thankfully the three of us made eye contact and that was enough to make Kerry, Sofia and I all members of the unspoken moment club.[16]

Over a school year, discounting the rainy days when I had to run across the paddock, or days when I was sick and didn't go to school, I experienced 600 minutes of free time in that paddock. Combine that with the time I spent alone in my bathroom, on average 20 minutes a day–that's 7300 minutes + the 600, which equals 7900 minutes of preparation. That's enough to fertilise a desire, so it becomes a need. A need that led me to the Norfolk boys–the board riders who sat under the Norfolk Island pines at the southern end of the beach.

Chapter 3

For years I'd hated the Norfolks. I just repeated what different parents said about them and pretended they were my views. By Year 8 I wanted to be like them, or be one of them, or at least sit close and eavesdrop. Instead of being 'lazy good for nothings', they appeared more like dolphins–intelligent and playful, cruising endlessly up and down the coast and frolicking in the green waves of summer. They wore their wetsuits to school, left salt in their hair to create tiny ringlets and spat up on the awnings in the bus shelters, yelling out 'beauty hot meal' when they caught the drips back in their mouths. I couldn't take my eyes off them. They were gods. They decreed what was acceptable and what was naff. To openly disobey them meant loss of property, physical injury and ridicule.

Unfortunately there was a longstanding rivalry between the surf club and the Norfolks. That was clear whenever I was on patrol. Every time the Norfolks saw me in a pair of Speedos and my patrol hat they'd point to my genitals and yell out 'check out Sandy's frankfurt and two new potatoes'. My only course of action was to retreat into the darkness of the patrol enclosure and hide until the trouble passed. It got to the point I wouldn't come out of the enclosure. If someone was drowning I'd have had a tough decision to make–save someone's life or face public humiliation.

Obviously my reluctance to be a team player was noted and I was asked to appear before Beach Ball, the surf club captain, who lectured me about my lack of commitment. If you could have drawn stripes on Beach Ball with neo-magics he'd have lived up to his name too. He told me about peer pressure and respecting my family, and he gave me a brochure on the EAC–the real estate cooperative where property listings are shared between many agents. He felt real estate could save me, telling me over and over he'd been in the buying and selling game for 25 years and it helped him to become a better person. 'In real estate you've got to respect everyone maaaaatey, otherwise it'll cost ya money. The next person you meet could be your next client.' He shook my hand so hard all the capillaries on his face rose to the surface like a geological map of the Menindee Lake system and then he said, 'Vigilance maaatey, vigilance'.

At that moment I would have gladly eaten the contents of an ashtray to get out of the surf club, but I'd have let my parents down if I did. I'd be dropping the cultural baton in the relay race of life. I wanted to be a Norfolk, but I still wanted to please my parents.

The past is like an experienced homing pigeon. No matter where you hide, it will find you again. It can be unsettling when you're trying to make a change and you're always listening for the flapping of pigeon wings.

I couldn't take my eyes off them.
They were gods.

Chapter 4

I had to create a situation where I could be absorbed by surfing. I didn't want to force my way in. I wanted to be asked. Being asked to do something makes you feel permanent.[17] When you're asked you get an ally, that is the person who asked you to join in. Still, you've got to put yourself in a position to be asked.

So every day in class I drew a surfboard, a Datsun Homer van and a road map that incorporated the north coast of New South Wales. I'd colour it in, stare at it, then imagine I was driving up the coast. I did this in the hope that others in the class would begin to associate me with board riding and not just the surf club. Sometimes I was so engrossed in my drawing I didn't even realise I was making a soft humming noise to represent the sound of the engine. That was until Stephen Cornish stabbed me in the thigh with a compass.[18] After that I was more careful about advertising my desires.

Once people knew I was interested in surfing, the next step was to get a surfboard. As I didn't have an income, buying one was out of the question. But I knew that my parents were having trouble knowing what to get me for Christmas. The microscope last year was not a winner, nor was the pool cue the year before. So in October when the inevitable questions about Christmas started up, I let it be known I wanted a custom-made surfboard. I also said I wanted it at the start of the school holidays, so it didn't look like a Christmas present. I wanted to give everyone the impression it was my third board.

As you get older Christmas is difficult to negotiate.* Parents always remember Christmas as a time when you were small. They hang on to that image of you as a tiny parcel of uncomplicated love shivering with excitement as you opened your beautifully wrapped presents, or the lonely uncle with nowhere to go except your house, holding a cheap cotton shirt against your back to see if it needed to be taken back. No one likes to ruin these images and when you play along you gain certain side benefits, such as superior presents, good word of mouth on the family grapevine, and so on. Sadly, I was in a position where I had to use this spirit of Christmas for my social advancement. Peer pressure is a far greater force than parental obligation.

Two weeks before the end of term a surfboard deal was presented to me in the car park at the airport. If there was ever a family discussion to be had it occurred at the airport. Every Sunday we'd go on a drive to look at renovations then end up watching the planes take off and land. We loved it. We'd all try and guess where each plane was going and what passengers were pleasure and which ones were business. Perhaps watching vulnerable people–happy arrivals and sad departures–helped stimulate the emotions which in turn promoted our family discussions.

The deal presented to me was as follows: 'You can have a surfboard, but no tantrums when it's haircut time, get your bronze medallion so you can save yourself if you're in trouble, and hang up your school clothes before dinner'.

---

* Sandman's Advice to the Unpopular, page 55

Chapter 5

It was the last week of Year 8 when Dad and I went to Braided Textures* to convert my paper desire into a reality. I would have rather gone by myself, but going with him was a necessary sacrifice–after all, it was a Christmas present.

I knew Dad wasn't sure about getting me a surfboard, but like most parents he knew if he could keep the quality enticements coming thick and fast I might stay at home longer. Some parents, like Nils's folks, made incredibly large investments to keep him at home–a swimming pool, a greyhound and a brand new car. Nils didn't have enough friends to make use of a swimming pool and instead of treating his greyhound mean to prepare it for racing it became his pet. Like many spoilt animals it had no road sense, and it got hit by a truck while chasing its favourite saliva-soaked ball onto the road. When they gave Nils his brand new car he left home the very next day. They should have bought him an older car so he wouldn't have got so far away so quickly.**

At Braided Textures it was a classic culture clash. A guy in faded jeans who smelled of bong water talking to a man dressed in a tailored blue suit with cuffed pants pulled up too high. To my surprise and my father's credit, he held his own by talking about his car. 'Cow of a tank on it. She bubbles back on ya. Ya never know when she's full. Noooo, she'll take a caravan up Bulahdelah.' I was so proud of him. He never spoke like that at home, or at work, but whenever

---

* Braided Textures was the name of a local boardmaker
** Sandman's Advice to the Unpopular, page 107

he was with a man, or group of men he didn't know very well, he dropped his g's and gave most objects a gender. As I got older I started to do it too.[19]

The board I chose was a 6 foot 6 inch, 17 inches wide with soft rails, a curved deck, thruster, twin fin, all white with a red stripe down the middle. The red stripe was my father's idea. He jokingly said the Civil Defence would be able to see me more easily from a helicopter with a distress signal painted on top. Here I was doing my best to act like an experienced surfer and my father was implying I couldn't surf. To cover up in front of the others I kept calling him by his first name, so we looked more like two brothers with a big age difference rather than a standard father and son.

The shaper said it would take two weeks for my board to be finished. I'd noticed that other boys getting boards custom made talked with the shaper, the glassier and so on, so whenever I went to check my board's progress I did the same. I had some awkward conversations, but I think it helped me to appear more 'seasoned'. The fact that there were always lots of bored-looking Norfolks hanging around, riding skateboards, pulling bongs and lighting farts didn't make life any easier for me either. I was envious of how uninhibited they were with each other.[20] Being bored looked like fun. That privilege seemed a few years away from me yet.

Despite the request for a red stripe the board turned out to be a pale lemon with no stripe. The shaper told me quite categorically that red and white had 'no vibe, man'. He was so confident. Perhaps the most confident teenager I'd ever met. I remember that as he showed me the colour he bit into some cheese and it made his gums bleed. At least my teeth were better than his. Apparently I've got strong saliva.* Every time I see a piece of cheese now I think of that guy's

---

* I've got only two fillings

gums. Every time I looked at my board I thought of cheese. When I thought of cheese I got hungry. When I eat cheese I get hay fever. When I get hay fever I think of cheese. When I think of cheese I picture the shaper's gums. One thing leads to another, but it always leads back to the original thing. You can never escape the past, but you can pretend it doesn't exist and that's how I dealt with the problem of the red stripe. I pretended we'd never asked for it and my anxiety disappeared. Perhaps my disappointment was simply stored somewhere else to be used at another time.[21]

NORFOLKS

Chapter 6

My getting a surfboard also coincided with one of the Norfolk boys, a guy called Mongrel, joining the army. If every beach or mall has a local god, then Mongrel was our god. Muscular, long black hair with bleached bits (courtesy of the salt and surf), a tan like the varnish on an old surf boat and, because of the fear factor, the most popular person in our area. He was the sort of guy who loved jumping off cliffs without warning, scraping his bum on the road while hanging on to the passenger door of a speeding car,* or tackling people on cement. Once for a bet he even ran through a plate glass window wearing a bike helmet. He loved to bleed and inflict pain on others, albeit by the nerve hold,[22] a dead leg,[22] or by hitting himself across the nose with the side of a ruler.**

Surfing wise, Mongrel was unique. He rode a red spear board with a tiny fin, so he slipped down the face of waves instead of going across them. He also surfed in a lumber jacket, board shorts worn over the top of pantyhose and a pair of old gym boots. Years later I learnt that he was allergic to jellyfish and he wore all that gear as a protective measure. At the time everyone thought it was a fashion statement and copied him. People would always gather to watch when he went in the water too, not just to see him carve up the waves, but to make sure he could swim in all that gear.

The first time I saw Mongrel was when I watched him feed a funnel-web spider that lived in the windowsill at the kiosk.

---

* *Sandman's Advice to the Unpopular*, page 88
** *Sandman's Advice to the Unpopular*, page 21

MONGREL PORTRAIT (ONE)

Myself and three others looked on in horror as Mongrel threw a fly into the funnel-webs' funnel web, causing it to appear from nowhere and snatch the panicked insect. A pet funnel-web spider is a very impressive pet. My only physical contact with Mongrel was when he flicked me with a beach towel rolled up like a kangaroo's tail.***

I knew Mongrel was going into the army because there was a big going away party for him on the same day I ordered my surfboard—three garbage bins full of beer, two car speakers sitting next to them on the sand pumping out Marvin

---

*** To make a kangaroo tail towel, you roll a beach towel from one corner to the diagonally opposite one. In the process the towel takes the shape of a Kangaroo's tail. When flicked it really hurts.

Gaye,[23] Neil Young and so on. Everybody was really drunk, spinning twice and jumping in the air after every slurp of beer. Girls danced as if they had broken ankles and boys head-butted beer cans, which left small cuts on their noses. If anyone vomited everyone cheered each convulsion like it was some type of achievement. One boy even tried to masturbate a fox terrier that lingered too long. Nils and I watched from behind a large cactus plant like two Prairie dogs.**** Thankfully my father was late picking me up that day, so we got to see everything, including Mongrel's wonderful speech.[24]

It was hard to say why Mongrel was joining the army. Perhaps he wanted to prove something to his mother, the handsome and hard working circular breather***** who ran the kiosk at the beach. Perhaps having a European background meant there was a deeper sense of family for him to emulate. Perhaps he thought it was cool. Perhaps he was drunk when he decided to join and now he was too embarrassed to go back on his word. Perhaps he was running away from an arranged marriage to a crane chaser. Perhaps it was all these things. At the time I didn't see any significance between my board and Mongrel joining the army.

**** *Sandman's Advice to the Unpopular, page 69*
***** *Sandman's Advice to the Unpopular, page 133*

Chapter 7

I was very excited the day I left Braided Textures with my surfboard, but the euphoria was short lived. As I walked past the panel beater's (next door to the board-maker's) all the tradesfolk stared at me and I was completely consumed by self-doubt. I untucked my shirt and tugged at my fringe to look more untidy, but their constant gaze was very unsettling. I knew that I'd have to work really hard at trying to feel more comfortable with a surfboard. I hadn't expected it to be so awkward.

However, as I climbed into my father's car my confidence grew. I knew that with a little luck and some practice this new arrival lying next to me on the fully reclined passenger seat could change my life. It certainly changed the atmosphere inside the car. The smell of resin filled the cabin and the light rain falling outside made it unpleasant to have the windows down for any length of time. To strike a happy balance between necessity and comfort, I spent that entire trip home winding the window up and down.

When we got home Dad parked very close to the wall, making it hard for me to get the surfboard out. I began to wonder if he'd done it on purpose, as if all these obstacles– the tradesfolk, the smell of resin–were a series of obstacles I'd have to overcome before I was a surfer. It was as if I was in a two-hour episode of the TV show *Kung Fu*–'When you remove the surfboard from the car you will be ready to leave home'. That's the way I saw it anyway.

Traditionally, when a task requires precision or patience I fail. The longer an obstacle endures the more doubt I create, and when I fail I cover my lack of success by celebrating the failure. However, on this particular day, as I struggled to get the board out of the car, I imagined my parents lying on the floor in the dining room, directly above the carport, watching me through tiny cracks in the floorboards, and that helped me to be patient.* Nowadays, to help with my concentration I always imagine I'm being watched by the people I need to impress.

Using my new-found determination, I got the board out of the car and disappeared into the rumpus room to look at it, smell it, and flick it with salty water (to see what it looked like when it was wet). I practised carrying it as well. I was

---

* Ironically, when I went upstairs that day both my parents had crumbs on their chests and thighs and their clothing was creased, so it added to the realism of what I had been imagining.

very interested to see if my back muscles twitched like Mongrel's when I picked it up and put it down again. I noticed some definition in my triceps if I wiggled the fingers holding the board, but I couldn't see my back properly so I couldn't verify any twitching of muscles there. Without movable wings on the mirror I couldn't see what was going on behind me.

Chapter 8

The next day, before loading my surfboard into the car for the maiden voyage to the beach, my mother insisted we take a photo. Every Christmas we sent out photos of us standing with our presents. As she desperately wanted us all in the picture and there was no timer on the camera, we had to ask the Gumleys (our neighbours) to help us.

Mr Gumley answered the door wearing a lap-lap and moccasins. I guess wearing this apparel was his idea of getting away from it all on a rostered day off. I remember thinking we should have phoned first because his eyes were very glassy and he had an Ovaltine moustache. Nevertheless appearances can be deceiving, because Mr Gumley did the job without complaint, even trading a few neighbour jokes along the way. For example: 'next time you come home drunk remember to open the gates before you drive the car in'.[25] After taking our picture he disappeared back to whatever it was he was doing. The sound of a gasoline powered engine starting up inside his house only added to the mystery of Mr Gumley's appearance that day.

As we motored towards the beach I wound the window down and let my mind wonder to Angourie, the sound of an inboard motor boat with a long wooden tiller and the image of a strong contemporary woman in a yellow crochet bikini. If I'm ever apprehensive about anything, this series of images always helps me to relax. Just as my dream woman was putting some saliva on her index finger, before wiping it along my bottom lip, an insect hit my eyelid and my daydream vanished. It was like an emotional wake-up call saying 'don't get too confident Sandy', because suddenly I remembered my father always dropped me opposite the Norfolk Island pines when he drove me to the beach. It was a habit he'd formed out of convenience because the road was wider near the pine trees and he didn't have to make a three-point turn. It was also where the Norfolk boys sat. They would see me get out of the car and I'd die another little social death. It's okay to be dropped off by a parent when you're in the surf club, respect for your elders is encouraged there–the firm handshake being the most popular way to show that respect. If you're a surfer, it's the opposite. You get a bus, scab a lift, but you never ever get a lift from a parent.

I didn't want to hurt his feelings by saying, 'I don't want to be seen with you. Drop me somewhere different'. I loved him.[26] So to cover myself I said I was hungry and that I wanted to get a steak sandwich from Newsomes Cafe. He thought it was strange ... 'seeing how you've just had 6 pieces of French toast with Holbrook's sauce for breakfast'. After a brief pause he added that it was actually quicker for him to get to work if he dropped me at Newsomes.

He told me to be waiting for him opposite the pine trees at 5pm. I'd imagined getting the bus home, but when his lips turned down at the sides and he touched his fringe with his middle finger, it was a sign the roller door was down.* He said it was his wedding anniversary and we were all going to the Copper Pot restaurant to celebrate, so he wanted to make sure that I was home on time. I secretly knew that, but I'd rather have my eyes filled with sand and the lids moved up and down than go to the Copper Pot. Nevertheless, I dutifully retreated like an inferior male monkey who'd lost a

---

* Sandman's Advice to the Unpopular, page 116

territorial dispute with an elder. I got my board out of the car and watched him disappear up the street. I couldn't watch him for too long because the path was hot and I'd left my thongs in the back seat.

Chapter 9

Usually when I get something new, like a pair of pants, they have to serve an apprenticeship first–get to know my other clothes, so to speak. So when people say 'New pants, Sandy?' I say 'Oh no, these are six months old'. New things are embarrassing. Old things are comfortable.

With my new surfboard there was no getting-to-know-you period at all. It was straight in at the deep end. I decided that if I saw anyone I knew I'd do what I'd practised in the rumpus room–wiggle the fingers holding the board, so my triceps danced like a big fat earthworm. That would make me seem playful and confident–like a dolphin. Unfortunately, it was so damn hot underfoot that every time my feet touched the ground, my bloody knees sprang up high like an enthusiastic AFL umpire. It was a shame, because I'd put a fair amount of energy into the triceps thing.

As I got nearer the surf I smelt the essence of coconut from the various suntan lotions and heard the screams of a girl being thrown in the whitewater by a boy she hadn't had sex with. I began to brew up a fresh batch of homemade doubt. Would my board be well received? Would I look odd carrying it? Food always helps me deal with anxiety, so when I reached Jim's Corner Store I remember thinking, 'I'd better buy a pie before I go across to the beach'.[27]

A man called Nigel owned Jim's. Nigel was a jockey-sized man with a cruelly distended nose who always sang a funny song about nature after every transaction.[28] He was the type of corner store chap who tried so hard to be nice it made his service extremely slow. I waited in the line to get my pie.

I'm good at waiting–I enjoy it.* It's an excellent hobby for those who aren't good with their hands.

From the corner of my eye I saw the three Lexies standing near a sunglasses carousel, all wearing identical lime-coloured crochet bikinis. I hoped they'd see me so I could impress them, but they were preoccupied, drinking milkshakes and pretending to look at sunglasses. When Nigel wasn't looking they each popped a pair of sunnies into their milkshake containers.[29]

The LEXIES

As Lexie One went past I flexed my fingers, sending my triceps into a wild dance, but she walked straight by me without so much as a glance. Lexie Two, on the other hand, stopped and stared at me like a tranquillised savanna animal. For a moment it appeared as if she was going to say something nice, so I leaned forward to listen, making sure I only looked at her forehead,[30] but instead of talking she sneezed twice on my face and that made the third Lexie laugh. Whenever Lexie Three laughed she made a loud snorting noise, which in turn made her laugh even more. I could imagine a time when Lexie Three would never be able to stop laughing. It made her the most likeable of the three Lexies, but her neverending loop of laughter, accompanied by the loud snorting noise, was certainly an Achilles heel in the Lexies' intimidating wall of cool. I wiped Lexie Two's nasal spray off my neck and watched her walk out of the shop.[31]

Nigel got a pie from the oven and squirted some sauce over the buttery lid. Before he handed it to me he sang his familiar transaction song. The fact that he also held your change away from you, so you had to lean over the counter and actually grab it from his hand, confirmed his rather unnatural need for affection.[32] Nigel certainly made the most of being trapped in a dark shop fourteen hours a day. I left his cave and went into the sunshine where I quickly ate my pie.* As I ground the buttery pastry into a gooey compound, it felt as if I was being hugged by a parent and I was instantly less anxious.

---

* Sandman's Advice to the Unpopular, page 34

Chapter 10

It's very important to pick the most fertile social soil for any period of rapid growth, so I studiously surveyed the coastal vista before deciding where to sit. The Norfolks were to my right, sunning themselves under the giant pine trees after their morning surf. The surf club was to my left. I could see Beach Ball hosing a slab of useless cement near the entrance to the club. Around the middle area were the Grommets—the worker ants, constantly running messages for the Norfolks, buying them hot chips, drinks, stealing money from unguarded clothing and taunting tourists to impress their older idols. I decided I'd sit to the right of the Grommets, hoping the rich social life between the Norfolks and the Grommets might wash down the hill and fertilise me in some form of emotional permaculture.[33]

The area I'd selected (a green council bench) was located on a bindi patch and a few of nature's little landmines stuck in my foot, causing me to perform a short but embarrassing modern dance. I think I covered the embarrassment because I acted like I meant to look stupid. I then placed my board in such a way it was highly visible to anyone using the path, sat back down on the bench and looked at the surf. My head would have seemed very still to anyone watching me, but my eyes were rotating wildly, trawling the beach for any interest in my board.

Eventually, after about an hour of sitting still, some of the Grommets stopped to check out my pale lemon 'stick'. I did a pterodactyl call to ensure their full attention. 'Cawwww!'[34] I'd recently decided to create an image of myself as someone who was slightly insane to help me find a niche.[35] Making seagull-like sounds, slapping my chest and licking a wall when anyone said 'Batman calling' were just some of the things I'd been trying out. I'd had quite a few requests for 'Batman calling'. The only problem was I often cut my tongue when I licked the wall. At any rate my noises made them look and that's the purpose of attention-seeking devices. They're good for attracting people and holding their attention while you think of something to say.

One of the Grommets, the one who looked like he'd been dragged up from the deep in a lobster pot and cooked on the spot, picked up my board and shook it, then threw it back onto the ground and said 'Piece of shit, man'. The board made a sickening sound as it struck the grass. I wanted to rush over and comfort it, but I thought, No Sandy, stay where you are—vulnerability is the doorway to humiliation. So I kept very still as they walked off towards the Norfolks, spitting every couple of paces like dogs marking out their territory. That's when I saw Mongrel—short hair, clean shaven and a set of sharp-looking sidelevers that made him look like Zorro.

piece of shit man

MONGREL PORTRAIT (TWO)

(NOTE TRICK CHARCOAL SIDE LEVERS)

I couldn't really see what was happening because he was surrounded by so many well-wishers. To get closer to him without drawing too much attention to myself I had to lie down on the grass and slowly roll over a few times, making my way up the fairly steep embankment by means of rotation. The grass had been recently mowed and I picked up a layer of clippings for my trouble. To someone hovering above me (such as Santa) I might have looked like a squat sausage being rolled in some breadcrumbs. A quick glance across the sky didn't reveal anyone looking at me. I guess I was the only one thinking that. The image you have of yourself is often different from the one others have of you.

The image you have of yourself is often different to the one others have of you.

It was strange to see Mongrel dressed in a shirt with buttons and pants with a belt. Closer inspection revealed his side levers weren't real, but painted on, perhaps the result of a cork being burnt and the charcoal residue being used like a make-up pencil. I'd seen the under-aged Grommets do a similar thing to get into pubs. I peered down to the kiosk where his mother worked, quickly trying to glue some possibilities together. I must have been looking away longer than I thought because when I glanced back up the hill the attitude of the Norfolks was completely changed. They'd scattered like umbrellas in an unexpected southerly and Mongrel was being chased by a guy in military attire. As Mongrel and the army guy disappeared down the side of a house with a big mulberry tree out the front, another MP stopped his car across the driveway and jumped out. He was so alert he appeared to be hovering a few centimetres above the ground.[36] I couldn't take my eyes off him.

Everyone waited for the MP and Mongrel to reappear. It probably wasn't that long a wait, but tension makes time go slower. Then, just as the pressure became unbearable, Mongrel, like a footballer exploding through a corporate banner, suddenly ripped through an oleander bush three doors down and bolted back across the road. Abuse and encouragement erupted from under the pine trees. This attracted the attention of the hovering guy who saw what was happening and raced down to assist his tiring colleague.

Mongrel now headed towards me, probably because I was standing slightly on the outside of the group.[37] I wished I had a manila folder so I could've pretended I was looking at important documents,* but before I had a chance to employ any tactics Mongrel and I were standing toe to toe. We were so close my private thoughts could have clung to his eyelashes. All I remember was his eyes were panicky,

---

* *Sandman's Advice to the Unpopular,* page 111

his chest was straining for air and his top lip was a mass of sweat bubbles. I'd thought endlessly about what to say if we ever met, but the best I could do was pick my teeth and stare at the ground. Then, in what appeared to be extra extra slow motion, he bent over, picked up my board and took off with it down the beach.

It was odd standing in front of a council bench (with 'Sandy takes it up the arse' carved on it), watching my board being taken away by a god who was in turn being chased by the military police. Initially I was worried that Mongrel might not bring the board back and my father would be angry. But as I watched him hit the boiling whitewater my thoughts changed to more practical matters. Did he like how the board felt under his arm? Did he like soft rails? Would it float him? Would it give him the power off the bottom he needed? Watching him push through the whitewater made me feel very proud and close to cool.

As Mongrel changed from wading to paddling the two MPs gained a little, but once they were knee deep in the whitewater their bulky military uniforms became heavy and Mongrel got away quite easily in the end. This realisation swept across the beach in the form of a cheer. I looked up the hill and smiled, too inhibited to cheer out loudly or pull the pants down like some of the other boys were doing. Nevertheless my board was being touched by the chest, stomach, pelvis and thighs of our god, so I had something in common with the Norfolks. I was connected to them.

Chapter 11

While Mongrel paddled about in the take-off area, cockily chatting with the flotilla of surfers who'd rushed out to support him, a strange thing happened. All the clubbies, sunbathers, fringe surfers, even the men who played shuttlecock on the hard sand,[38] people who had been coming to the beach for years and never spoken to each other, started forming discussion groups to watch Mongrel's great escape unfold. His act of defiance had united the entire beach, removing all the impenetrable social barriers that stop unconfident people from intermingling. Civil disobedience can eradicate borders and here was proof. I, Sandman, was standing in amongst the Norfolks for the first time ever. Instead of my pants being removed and thrown onto the roof of the kiosk, my shirt stuffed with coleslaw, or my bag covered in cocks and balls, I was one of them—a bulbous piece of green kindling sitting precariously on the Norfolks' impressive social bonfire.

I'd always tried to imagine what it felt like to stand under the giant Norfolk Island pines at the southern end of the beach surrounded by the coolest people in the area. Well, it felt good. Very good. For the record there was spongy grass, no bindies, both sexes were well represented, most of the men were more attractive than me (I was too embarrassed to make lengthy eye contact with the women) and if you took two giant steps forward and leaned on the fence you were spitting distance from the public change sheds. (And I thought I was getting shat on by seagulls.)

I stood on the outside of the group's inner circle for about an hour.[39] I couldn't focus on one thing long enough to understand it, nor did I have the confidence to try anything flamboyant. The only impressions I made on the Norfolks lasted no longer than a breath. I simply moved my lips to give people the impression I was contributing to the conversation and I tried to laugh when the others laughed, so it looked as if I had the same sense of humour as everybody else. 'That's my board' and 'He's got my board' were probably the only things I said that resembled conversation. I was like a fourth grade cricketer suddenly promoted into the Test team.

I, Sandman, was standing in amongst the Norfolks for the FIRST TIME EVER.

Chapter 12

As the siege entered its second hour the numbers under the pine trees dwindled, because most Norfolks paddled out to be with their god. Those Norfolks who didn't–Melon, who allegedly once ate a cockroach for ten dollars; Neville, a ginger-haired boy with blisters on the lips; and Spud, barred from all clubs in the district for letting off the fire extinguishers (along with myself)–formed a discussion group. With fewer people under the pines there was more space for a chap with soft hands and the comic timing of a walnut to manoeuvre in.

TWO NORFOLKS

a mullet cut

Melon   Neville
(FROM "THE HOUSE THE COAST MONGREL")

The MPs were now standing outside the surf club talking to Beach Ball. Their conversation went for some time and it had the attention of every person on the beach. My discussion group speculated about what they were saying. The most popular suggestion was they were trying to get Beach Ball to lend them the jet boat. You could tell from the body language that the talk was not going well. In fact it became quite heated, which resulted in Beach Ball giving them the 'forks' as they walked away. I immediately turned to Melon and said 'If you want I can go down to the club and find out what happened'. Gossip and secrets give you power.[40]

Well, I couldn't get to the surf club fast enough. I didn't sprint because excessive displays of emotion are naff, so I pictured myself as a West Indies cricketer coming into bowl and that gave me a certain fluidity and covered the fact I was quite frantic. My demeanour turned to panic though when I got into the surf club and found that Beach Ball was in the toilet. It was common knowledge in the surf club movement that Beach Ball was a 40 minute man. All men involved in beach culture are legends for something: driving a car from the back seat at high speed, diving off the mast of a ship in the Whitsundays, anonymous acts of kindness, or in Beach Ball's case, sitting on the toilet for an incredibly long time. I couldn't afford to wait 40 minutes. I had a mission that had to be completed, so I walked down the long hall of cubicles until I reached the unmistakable odour of our club captain.

'Beach Ball,' I said.

'Piss off.'

'It's Sandy.'

'Piss off.'

Usually if I'm rejected I fold, but on this day I persisted.

'What happened between you and the military guys?'

'Piss off.'

'Come on.'

'If I tell you will you go away?'

'Yes.' I knew how awful it was to be interrupted in the toilet but I had to know what Beach Ball talked about with the MPs.

'They want me to stop people going in the water, so they can isolate the dickhead on the board.'

'Thank you.' I'd always been taught to say thank you to elders. I'd also been instructed to always return my window to the closed position and lock my door after receiving a lift. A passenger door left unlocked says a lot about a person.[41]

Chapter 13

    I arrived back at the pines around the same time as a group of surfers who'd been 'out the back' with Mongrel and four extra MPs who'd just pulled up across the road. Despite the commotion all eyes fixed on me. I checked around my neck to be sure I didn't have a piece of cucumber stuck there* or a Kick Me sign pinned to my back. To be looked at by so many cool people at once was unsettling. I tried to use awkwardness to my advantage. Sometimes uncertainty can make you look bohemian and interesting. Nevertheless, I remember enjoying the intoxicating effect the attention was having on me.[42] I got a little greedy knowing I had quality information to impart and I think I let the gap in the conversation get unnaturally long. Sadly, I had to break the tension by saying 'They're going to try and stop people going into the surf'. Well, I cannot remember a time when something I said made a bigger impact.

Mongrel, according to those surfers who'd just returned from being with him, was hungry and cold. (He'd been out nearly three hours.) So the plan was to buy him some food, put it in watertight containers, along with a wetsuit, and paddle it out to him. To make that easier to achieve it was suggested the Grommets should create a diversion on the sand to distract the MPs.[43] If Mongrel could stay out until nightfall he could then paddle round to the breakwater under the cover of darkness and from there it would be easier to get away. The only problem was, nightfall was a good seven hours off yet.

---

* *Sandman's Advice to the Unpopular*, page 12

Chapter 14

As the siege entered its fourth hour and the novelty wore off, some Norfolks started to question my presence under the pines. Who's the guy with too much hair on one side of his head?* Spud, rather surprisingly, defended me, telling the others I had an interest in the situation–'Mongrel's got his board, man'.[44, 45] I was touched, but it led to the suggestion I should be one of the people to paddle the stuff out to Mongrel. I said, 'I'd be more happy creating a diversion'. Melon said, 'Bad luck. The Grommets are already doin' something, man'.

A wave of fear swept over me. I did a pterodactyl to buy a little thinking time. I didn't get many laughs, but it was laughter nonetheless. I'd never ridden a surfboard. There was no way I could paddle out the back. Secondly, if I got the board back my connection to the Norfolks would disappear. Thirdly, if I didn't get the board back my father would be angry. Fourthly, if I refused to do it I'd look like a chicken. Instinctively I felt option three was my best bet. Act like I couldn't give a shit about my board and deal with my father later. So I said, 'I don't give a shit about my board'. Unfortunately the conversation had moved on and I just looked stupid.

I offered to help Spud buy the food from Jim's, hoping that if I helped now they'd forget about me taking the food out to Mongrel later. I also thought if I could talk to Spud privately he might speak to the others on my behalf. Spud didn't want

---

* Sandman's Advice to the Unpopular, page 103

me to go to the shop with him (you can't get more definite than pushing someone away), but the thought of paddling a surfboard in front of the Norfolks helped me overcome the rejection. However, as we left I was pleasantly surprised when one of the Norfolks yelled out 'Do the bird call again, man'. I immediately obliged, blurting several pterodactyls in succession. The reaction wasn't huge, but I remember thinking, If I persist with this line of behaviour I'll catch on here.

At Jim's Spud and I pushed past several people waiting to be served as if we were royalty. In some ways the Norfolks were royalty. They belonged to the 'House of Coast Mongrel' and one of the privileges of being a royal was not lining up in shops and stealing hot chips off people who couldn't surf. When a lady with two children complained to Nigel that we'd pushed in front of her, Spud told me to pull his finger, which I did, and he 'blew off' then looked at me as if to say I did it. I must admit I felt uncomfortable being a rebel. I wanted to be wild, but it didn't come naturally to me. I tried to apologise to the lady using just my eyes because I didn't want Spud to see me. From the ferocious way she told me to get lost[46] I must have looked a little lecherous.

We bought a salad bun, six summer rolls, a fruit juice and some assorted sweets. When Nigel sang his cloying song Spud stopped him mid-verse and said, 'Eh Nig, stick your song up your arse, man'. I laughed even though I didn't find it that funny. I was just supporting Spud because I think he thought he'd been quite funny.

Chapter 15

As we walked back towards the pines (my knees springing up high again due to the hot tar) I asked Spud why Mongrel had gone AWL. 'Whaddya reckon? He fuckin' hated it, man.'

Spud sped up a little and I had to put a little more vigour into my gait to keep up. 'Why'd he join then?' I said, wanting to know more about my god. 'His old girl' man. She wanted him to do something with himself, so he joined the fuckin' army, man.' Mongrel? Worried what his mother thinks? My lips must have moved because Spud asked me who I was talking to. That was something I had to work on. Not moving my lips while I was thinking. Then Spud said, 'Don't ask me any more questions, man'. I knew exactly what he meant. He didn't want the others to see me talking to him. I could understand his position. I'd been dreading running into Nils and his parents all morning. Every Saturday Nils and his parents went to the beach to sunbake and they always ended up talking to me for hours. The last thing I needed on this day was to be standing with the Norfolks then have Nils and his parents come up to me and talk about MusicaViva.[47] I liked them, but I had to protect my own interests. I couldn't afford to be seen with people so far down the food chain. Likewise Spud with me. So I picked my teeth, stared at the ground and tried to pretend Spud hadn't said what he said.

Chapter 16

Obviously the word had got around about the siege because there were people standing two and three deep on the embankment and still more folk were arriving. Cars and people everywhere. This was the biggest Saturday crowd since the Governor-General drove a silver-plated bulldozer into the old retaining wall to start the beach improvement scheme. The Grommets were having a field day, letting down tyres and wiping dog turds on windscreen wipers. 'When it rains you know somewhere someone is very angry.'

By the time we got back with the food the MPs were on the sand stopping people from entering the water. I felt quite good that my information had turned out to be correct, but on the other hand I was still frantically trying to think of an alternative to my paddling out to Mongrel. Someone had already obtained a wetsuit and the watertight containers were apparently on their way, so if it was going to happen it would be soon.

I needed a space to collect my thoughts without the pressure of trying to please those further up the food chain. I also needed to talk to the Grommets and find out about their plan. I employed the $3 Escape Technique, which involved dropping coins on the ground and pretending to chase them.[48] At the time, I thought I'd managed to make quite a natural-looking break from the group. In retrospect, I needn't have sacrificed three dollars' worth of loose change because no one was looking at me. Still, it's better to be safe than sorry.

I slipped behind a large Fijian flame tree, took off my board shorts and rolled my Speedos low (that's how you could tell a Norfolk from a fringe board rider). Then I walked down the embankment and began to look for the Grommets. I stuck close to the walls or hugged their shadows to stay out of view.[49, 50] As long as they couldn't see me, I wouldn't have to paddle out.

The kiosk was doing a roaring trade. People were five deep waiting for hot chips and dagwood dogs. The longer Mongrel could stay in the water, the more money his mother would make. I'm sure he must have seen the lines of people in the kiosk too. I guess he was doing her proud and in a way that suited him. For years I'd tried to please my parents while he rejected his. Now I was trying to reject mine and he was trying to please his. Mongrel and I almost had something in common.[51]

I found the Grommets inside the kiosk. They were busy spreading bindies over the floor, so little children would tread on them. They called in their Cyclical Nature of Irritation Technique. It was cyclical because to stop the children screaming and inflaming the already tense atmosphere inside the kiosk the parents had to take them outside. It was irritating because when the children realised they weren't getting any chips they started screaming again, and Daddy would have to line up once more. It was a technique since the Grommets did the same thing every week. Some of their methods were cruel, but they certainly showed a deep understanding of human behaviour.

Before I had time to attract the Grommets' attention, let alone ask about what they were planning, the Norfolks started whistling. It was some form of prearranged signal because all the Grommets stopped what they were doing and ran off. When the Norfolks saw I was there too, they called out to me as well. It was nice to have my name yelled by the

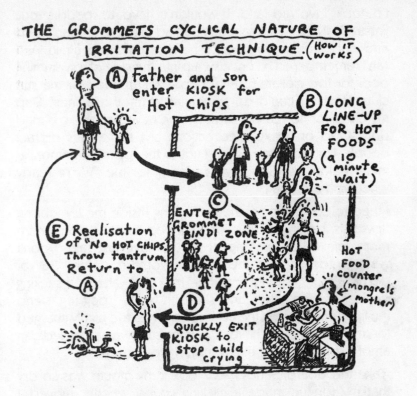

THE GROMMETS CYCLICAL NATURE OF IRRITATION TECHNIQUE. (HOW IT WORKS)

(A) Father and son enter KIOSK for Hot Chips

(B) LONG LINE-UP FOR HOT FOODS (a 10 minute wait)

(C) ENTER GROMMET BINDI ZONE

(E) Realisation of "NO HOT CHIPS." Throw tantrum. Return to (A)

(D) QUICKLY EXIT KIOSK to stop child crying

HOT FOOD COUNTER (mongrels' mother)

Norfolks, but it made my heart speed up, my breathing shallow and I felt abnormally light-headed. I'd had anxiety attacks before, like when I discovered a lump in my vas deferens the size of a marble and I thought I'd never see thirteen.* The only thing that calmed me down that night was breathing into a paper bag and eating a sandwich. So I rummaged through a nearby bin and found a paper bag. I also saw the remains of a sandwich. If there hadn't been ants on it I might have eaten it.

Once my breathing stabilised I chased after the Grommets. If I could attach myself to them and do whatever they did,

---

*The lump turned out to be a sebaceous cyst which required minor surgery.

I'd look involved and I wouldn't have to paddle out. Frustratingly they were already up and over the embankment, and once you're isolated it's hard to catch up again. As I ran I remembered I'd once swam into the side of a swimming pool for five dollars to avoid collecting money for the surf club. Maybe I could do something along those lines? Slap my chest for no reason, or eat some newspaper like a mad dog? Odd or unexpected actions can sometimes distract people. Unfortunately, when I got to the top of the embankment Melon and Spud were waiting for me. 'We're ready when you are, shag.'

I tried to cover the southerly brewing inside me by looking upwards, making my eyelids look heavier, thus giving me a more relaxed appearance. I should have just said 'I don't want to do it', but the words wouldn't come. Out of desperation I strung together my best attention-seeking devices–the haaatherear,[52] skeleton teeth,[52] peg leg,[52] and the lip trumpet[52]–but the atmosphere was too highly charged for my offerings to have any impact. I was stranded. An amphibious creature that'd misjudged the tide.[53]

'Take this board, Sandy.' As I took it my mouth was so dry that my tongue made a clicking sound when it moved. I sounded like Skippy trying to open a set of French doors in a house fire. I was cornered with only two options–humiliate myself or be humiliated.

Chapter 17

I guess what happened next is similar to what a drunk yobbo experiences when he or she is about to streak across the SCG during a Test match. A moment appears before you and you snatch it. You don't think about it, you just do it.

Without warning a lid blew off my inhibitions and I was soaked in overconfidence. I moved to what could be best described as an imaginary fence. I put a leg over, my foot touched the ground where only the champions tread, a shiver of greatness slithered up my spine and into my brain like a tree snake. Then the snake of overconfidence coiled itself around my secret desires, sent a message to my other leg–'come on over the water's fine'–and for better or worse away I went.

I ran down a path and across a section of grass that led onto the sand. The only reason I knew I was changing locations was the texture underneath my feet was changing every few metres. I was locked into some type of dream state.[54] Onlookers reacted with a mixture of hysteria and bewilderment. I could tell they wanted me to succeed by the way they yelled at me as I ran past them. I bet they wanted me to fall flat too. After all, that's the Australian way. The emotion I was experiencing at this point was being pumped up from a very private place deep inside me. It made watching me rather like watching two people having sex under a towel on a crowded beach. You shouldn't look, but you can't help it because privacy is so compelling.

Suddenly this internal force fired my legs to go even faster and the two almighty flesh pistons underneath me started to pump and push me towards the 'other side'. On the other side I could see remarkableness, perhaps a hotel for legends to live in rent free. A voice inside screamed, 'There it is, Sandy.' Go for it!'

'Yes, I see it. I see it.'

'Run to the tunnel of greatness, Sandy.'

'Yes! Yes!'

Desperation controlled everything now. It ripped off my shirt, my swimmers too. 'You're nude,' cried the voice. 'What about a little comedy?'

I let my hands trail behind me like two fishing nets scooping up my afterglow. I was a commercial trawler. 'Look at those people laughing at me. I can do anything I want. I'm an aeroplane.' I made an engine noise and stuck my arms out like they were wings.

'There's the tunnel, Sandy.'

'I see it.'

'Go Sandy, go. Be free little magpie!'

Suddenly I felt a terrible pain across my face. A warm wet feeling on my lips. The ground was looming up towards me, so quickly I couldn't even get my hands into a position to break my fall. As I hit the sand the wind went out of me like a fresh bottle of Pepsi being opened. I felt a giant weight on my stomach. I remember I screamed out 'Get that brick off me! Get it off!' Then everything went quiet.

Chapter 18

An eeriness follows an earthquake and as the adrenalin subsided I experienced that eeriness. People were crowded around staring at me. This must be what it's like to have charisma. I had a picture of myself as someone who was lying on their back on wet sand. As I looked down towards my toes I realised I was lying on my back on wet sand. My bulbous frame did not please me either–my stomach was higher than my chest. Why could I actually see my stomach? Slowly a mist began to clear. A quick wipe of the lips revealed the wet sensation I'd felt was blood trickling from a cut on my top lip. The brick on my stomach was Beach Ball's knee. I looked up at him and said, 'What happened?'

He leaned forward and whispered like a cartoon snake, 'You've been a bad bad puddycat Ssssssandy.'

Then he got me up and briskly walked me towards the surf club. Most of the crowd seemed to follow us. Some were making engine noises with their mouths. I was also nude, but that hadn't really sunk in either.

I saw Spud, Melon and some other Norfolks beaming at me. So excited they were their eyebrows were going up and down like caterpillars about to hatch. I asked Spud, using my eyes, 'Did you make it out to Mongrel?' He just smiled and made an engine noise with his mouth.

Chapter 19

The odour of blocked drains, smelly toilets and the faint hum of men's dirty talk inside the surf club was familiar enough to make me feel comfortable. Beach Ball suggested I have a shower while he rang my father. He said he'd try to find me some clothes too. He paused before he left the room.

'You should know that some people have formally complained about you, maaateyy. I think when you made the sound of an aeroplane and spun ya dick around like it was a propeller you might have gone a little too far, maaateyy.'

'I don't remember that.'

'Oh yes,' said Beach Ball, 'quite a show. I'll give ya the cork tip'. Then he left, leaving the club's boat sweep to keep an eye on me. I hated the idea of my offending people. I started to feel sick about it. I'd have to get their phone numbers and make it up to them. What could I do? Mow their lawns? Wash their cars? I wonder what the Norfolks thought? Did Beach Ball say he was ringing my father? Did I create a diversion or what? My hands were shaking so much I had trouble operating the shower taps and I took a nasty blast of boiling hot water on my chest. Sometimes a little twitch has big ramifications. This one cost me a red chest. Had I really run across the beach pretending to be an aeroplane?

After my shower I was returning to the change room and suddenly there he was, Mongrel, my god, sitting on a bench, head bowed, looking like he'd been lost in the Blue Mountains for several years. An MP whose eyebrows joined in the middle was standing over him and my board was lying on the floor in front of him. I tentatively smiled at Mongrel, hoping my warmth would engage him, but I might as well have been the Channel Ten news the way he avoided looking at me. It was very disheartening. When I nodded at the MP he smiled back and made an engine noise with his mouth. The boat sweep made the same noise. To give the impression I didn't care I made the noise too and everyone (except Mongrel) smiled. Obviously the Norfolks had failed to reach Mongrel. Obviously I had failed to create a big enough diversion. At least I wouldn't have to paddle a surfboard out.

When there's a long silence there's always an expectation to say something clever. I thought I'd better move around a little to offset this expectation. If you're not moving you're not interesting.[55] Again, the fact I was nude made the situation very awkward. So I coughed. A dry nervous one. A cough can sometimes be a conversation starter, but not this day. Mongrel looked up all right, but his stare completely paralysed my lips and we plunged back into the land of the long white middle-class silence.

'I ... I ... ran across the beach nude.' Even though no one had asked me a question I was very happy with the way that particular sentence came out. I turned my head to the side to congratulate myself. 'Well done, Sandy. You're going well, Sandy.' I must have moved my lips again because Mongrel said 'What?' Being self conscious is so tiring sometimes. You're always looking at yourself. It's like having two people to feed. Myself and myself.

Thankfully two MPs entered with Mongrel's mother and that saved me from answering the question. Mongrel's mother was a striking woman, a big shock of black hair, big eyes, a squat yet vivacious figure, but she always looked tired. This day was no different. Mongrel stood up and hugged with his mother for a long time. I noticed he was clutching her much harder than she was clutching him.[56] The scene was quite emotional and the rest of us in the room didn't know where to look. Whenever situations get emotional I get the giggles. This day was no different.

I felt I should receive some credit for my part in her record takings, so I stood up said something like 'Eh, that was my board you had out there'.

Mongrel stopped hugging, looked at me as if I'd rudely interrupted and said, 'It's a piece of shit, man'.

Chapter 20

There were still quite a few people standing around watching as Mongrel was pushed into the army vehicle and whisked away. As the car sped off, the Grommets chucked rocks and cans at it. Naturally once the main attraction left the crowd thinned, so Beach Ball and I took the opportunity to make a beeline for my father's car. Thankfully, Beach Ball's rotund shape shielded me from being spotted in the 'I escaped from Dubbo Gaol' T-shirt he'd found for me in Lost Property.

Beach Ball said he'd told my father I'd been hit by the board. He recommended that I stick to that story. I said jokingly, 'Maybe you don't want him to know it was your arm that caught me across the face when you tackled me from behind, eh?'

He moved in very close to my face, so close that I could see bits of partly chewed food in his teeth, and he said, 'I scratch your back, you scratch mine maaateyyy'. To be honest, I was glad he hadn't told my father the truth.

I felt like a native animal that had been caught, tagged and was about to be released back into the wild by a ranger. I couldn't wait to scurry off and hide in my established pattern of behaviour.

Chapter 21

As my father and I waited to make a right-hand turn onto the main coast road (all the roads were clogged with traffic because of the siege), I slid down in the seat to make myself less visible, just in case someone yelled, 'There's the guy that ran across the beach nude pretending to be an aeroplane'.

'You all right?' my father said with fatherly warmth.

'Not bad,' I replied.

'Beach Ball said you were hit in the head.'

'I'm a lot better now thanks.'

It was starting to rain. I could see the Norfolks huddled together under the pine trees. They looked miserable. I was dry, warm and mobile. Seeing them worse off than me made me feel much better. It felt like I'd had a win. It wasn't a bad day after all. I'd been under the Norfolk Island pines, got a few laughs, been to the shop with Spud. I'd seen Mongrel ride my board, I'd seen the entrance to the tunnel of greatness, and my parents would never know that I'd run across the sand nude pretending to be an aeroplane. That is, unless Nils' parents had seen me. I rested my hand on the board and thought, Well done, board.

My father said, 'What?'

'Nothing.'

'I thought you said something.'

'No.'

'How was the board?'

'Good. Very good.'

'That's good.'
I started to think about the 14 prawn fritters I always ordered at the Copper Pot and any lingering anxiety about the day disappeared. That was until my father said, 'You know you'll have to wear your tan suit to dinner'.

The Ordinary Prince
in the Special tan suit...

*R*eference Section

The Reference Section is made up mostly of pieces that I have presented on the breakfast show at Triple J between 1994 and 1996.

1 Artistic impression

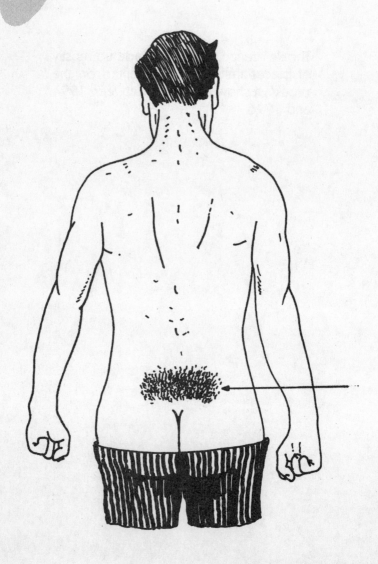

2 Lie down in your bathroom to look more relaxed

I enjoy being alone in my bathroom, sitting on my toilet, or lying on the ground letting the cool of the tiles soothe my skin. If I'm disturbed while I'm in my bathroom it feels like someone has put their hand inside my soul and taken something private from me. It can give you quite a shock too, and when you're shocked you do embarrassing things.

Last year I had a handyman at my garden flat liberating some windows that were stuck. Most of the time he was there I was in the toilet, engrossed in a game where I use two pencils to represent two athletes competing. Suddenly he slid open the bathroom door. I was so shocked by the intrusion, my legs flung apart, my hands opened as a defensive measure and my two pencils fell into the toilet. Not only was I humiliated to be caught playing such an immature game, but I'd had those pencils since I was ten and now they were gone forever. So I asked the handyman to put translucent glass in my bathroom door and convert my toilet bowl into a banana chair, so I could go to the toilet lying down and be able to see if someone was coming in advance. Now if I'm ever surprised in the bathroom, I have time to prepare a calm expression for my face and, thanks to my banana chair toilet seat, my body shape looks relaxed. I may look stupid, but I can live with that.

3 Possessiveness can cause rust

When Nils's mother scratched the duco off my silver coupe, I was undecided whether I should invoice her for the damage or forget about it. Although it was a deliberate act on her part, the damage wasn't done in anger. It was done with affection, and that's what made it hard for me to decide.

Nils is from a close-knit family, so close he was not allowed to go anywhere without his parents. He didn't see the city at night until he was over twenty. So as you can imagine, Nils's mother was quite emotional when I arrived to pick him up and take him on our end of year trip. Personally, I didn't think two nights in Kiama was such a big deal.

Everything was under control until we started to move off. If our progress hadn't been hindered by a series of speed humps (they were like driving over wombats) I probably could have got the car over 20 k and shaken her off. Once she was in arm's length of my car she pounded the boot with her fist, pleading with me to stop and let him out. Nils said she developed leg speed at school running down the boys who used to tease her about being a socialist. Her wedding ring combined with her powerful forearms did a real number on my duco. Her possessiveness let the rust in, but it was my procrastination that let it ruin a fine vehicle. Act swiftly to combat possessive behaviour. Especially if you live near the ocean.

4 *Possessiveness advertises frailty*

At the front of my garden flat there's a family of Willie wagtails. During their nesting season they seem to attack anything that comes even remotely close to the nest. Birds, cats, a three-legged dog who when he barks appears to be saying 'Norman', and people with wet hair and crisp eyebrows. In fact, they go off so often they're like a neon sign saying 'there's a Willie wagtail nest up here with four eggs in it, help yourself'. It was sad when the magpies raided their nest, but I couldn't help thinking that if the wagtails had been less vocal in their protective measures no one would have even known about the nest.

Nils's parents were the same. Every weekend they'd hover in the front yard, his dad pretending to build a rockery, his mother trimming cypress pines to resemble their ancestors. Any child who dared to venture near their house got a blast from the hose. All this did was make people more curious about Nils and subsequently he became a prized target at school. No student had more texta cock and balls on their schoolbag than Nils. By protecting him so vehemently, his parents were actually advertising his frailty.

5 My Serenade

From the club the boys file out into the autumn air. Some rev cars, some clutch beers, some just linger on the stairs. From a park I watch a fight. The same two guys that fought last night. That's when I think you, my dear Virginia.

I park the car up by the school, creep in past your swimming pool. Down the path your father made. I'll wake you with my serenade. You will think I'm crazy and you'll love me again Virginia.

I crawl along your flowerbox. I tap upon your windowpane. I whisper I love you and gently I say my name. Then I sing my alcoholic serenade.

Do you still have the stars in your eyes?
Do you still wear my leather ring?
Do you still sing our favourite song?
I say your first name whenever I can.

From up above a head pops out, a face I do not recognise.

A voice yells down 'What's going on?' 'I'm serenading Virginia.' The voice yells back 'that family's moved, there is no Virginia in that room'.

6 *I wish I'd waited until I was more mature before I had my first sexual encounter*

My first sexual encounter was rather public. It was in a park, next to a picnic hut. There was even a path about 10 metres away, but thankfully we were shielded by a row of oleanders, or nature's French doors, as my uncle Nev called them. It was also a little soggy because there was a tap that couldn't be turned off and the run-off had raised the watertable to such a level it made the back of my Midford cotton shirt quite damp.

Despite all this inconvenience, the frenzy that lust brings overrode these geographical inadequacies. We simply had to find somewhere, and fast. The big problem was my lack of maturity. If I'd been older I'd have had a car and I wouldn't have had to attach my pushbike to my ankle with a raincoat in case it got stolen while I was too randy to notice. We were in a high-risk crime area, especially on Thursday night shopping, so it was a precaution I had to take. Any sudden movement dragged the bike towards me and that was often enough to ring the bell, thus I got distracted. It was like I was dragging my childhood into my adolescence. Needless to say, I had a few boy's problems that night. At least it was quick.

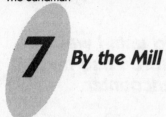

7 By the Mill

I hate to get up early, get into my car.
I hate to see my friends a'surfing while I spend my day a'working. I always wept on my way to work.
I cried into my locker as I changed from civvy clothes.

The saddest sounds are the sounds of industry.
You have to shout just to make a word.
You can't make friends if you can't be heard.

I used to get so lonely being at the mill. The toilet was the only place I ever went where everything went still.
But when they finally caught me, they said they'd dock my pay. So underneath the cranes a'crunching, that's where I will stay.

But by the Mill near the fitters' shop! There's a piece of paradise there.
By the mill near the fitters' shop! We all grew tomatoes there.
By the mill near the fitters' shop! We slept on sheets of cardboard there.
By the mill near the fitters' shop! I met a Turkish man who always shared his lunch with me.

The saddest case I ever saw was a Tally clerk.
He hated being married so he always stayed at work.
When we finally got him to come to the Fitter's shop, we asked him many questions and about his life we learned.

the Mill

page 1.

I hate to get up ear-ly get in-to my car I hate to see my friends a surfing

while I spend my day a work-ing oh I al-ways wept

on my way to work I cried in-to my lock-er as I changed from civvy clothes the

sad-dest sounds are the sounds of in-dus-try the sad-dest sounds

are the sounds of industry you have to shout just to make a word you

can't make friends if you can't be heard oh no---

I used to get so lone-ly be-ing at the mill the toi-let was the on-ly place where

every-thing went still but when they fin-'lly caught me they said they'd dock my pay so

under-neath the cranes a - crunching that's where I will stay the sad-dest sounds

are the sounds of in-dus-try the sad- dest sounds are the sounds of industry you

have to shout just to make a word you can't make friends if you

can't be heard but

The Sandman

page 2.

By the mill near the fit-ters shop (I)   1 Theres a piece of par-a-dise there
                                          2 We all grew to-ma-toes there
                                          3 We slept on sheets of card-board there

met a Turk-ish man who al-ways shared his lunch with me

met a Turk-ish man who said that this job was not the go----

The sadd-est case I ever saw was a tal-ly clerk he

hat-ed being married so he always stayed at work but

when we fin-'ly got him to come to the fit-ters shop we

asked him ma-ny ques-tions and about his life we learned the

70

8 *Why first home owners often have stooped shoulders*

I was working in real estate with a red-headed man who looked like Elvis and one day we were listing a nice three-bedroom place when the vendor said, 'I'll show you the downstairs flat before you leave. My family lives there'.

'Isn't this a one-storey place?' I replied.

'No! No! We have a lovely flat underneath.'

So we all (the vendor, my boss and myself) went down the side of the house and stopped at a small door. The vendor knocked twice and when we heard a faint 'come in', he pushed the door open. The first thing I saw was a woman in her late thirties hunched over a stove. The roof was so low that the back of her neck and the top of her shoulders were resting against the ceiling. As she turned her head to welcome us her left cheek pressed up against the ceiling. She said she'd prefer it if we didn't go into the bedroom because the twins were asleep. The vendor chipped in, 'It is small, but we own it and that's the main thing. The tenants upstairs almost cover the mortgage'.

As we were leaving I said to my boss the flat wouldn't be a selling point because it wasn't council approved. He said he thought the house would sell anyway because 'this guy'll take whatever he can get'.

'How can you tell?' I said.

'The stooped shoulders on his wife.'

9 Maintaining a rage can be obsessive

In Year 4 my teacher found out I followed the North Sydney Rugby League team. She told me she was a also fan of Norths and that she knew some of the players, so she could get me some souvenirs. The next week when she gave me a pair of Jim Schroder's football socks I was quite touched, but I was also underwhelmed because I didn't know who Jim Schroder was. (I later learned he was a front rower with North Sydney in the sixties.)

When I got home I showed the socks to my mother. She was worried about hygiene and said, 'Never wear other people's socks'. Then she threw them out. Under the cover of darkness I retrieved them and hid them under some loose parquetry floor tiles behind the lounge, along with the sexy pages I'd torn out of Dad's copy of *Valley of the Dolls*. Normally I wouldn't combine sex with anger, but there were no other loose floor tiles behind the lounge. The image of my mother throwing out the socks and me fetching them again was a much repeated scenario during my teen years. Recently, when one of the socks blew out of my car, I was so concerned I retraced my steps until I found it again. When I finally picked up the soggy sock and looked at it closely, I realised my relationship with Jim's socks had become a tad obsessive. After all, I now lived alone and didn't derive the same pleasure in telling my mother I still had his socks.

10  *The Magpie Is My Favourite Bird*

I was deeply touched one day in May,
When some magpies came to play.
I stared at them through curtains drawn
While they played upon my lawn.
I kept very quiet, so I'd not disturb
The playful qualities of the magpie bird.

Each magpie took its turn
To jump into a basket.
In and out they hopped
With much magpie laughter.
The scene was so supportive, uninhibited and warm,
the day the magpies played so freely on my lawn.

The magpie is my favourite bird,
With a communal sense that's quite superb.
That is why the magpie is my favourite bird.

11 *Keeping happy cost me money*

As I strolled along the waterfront one day I saw a fleet of inboard motor boats for hire. Each one was named after one of the seven dwarfs–Sneezy, Happy, etc. At first I thought, what a cloying and irritating concept. But as I was feeling down (earlier, at the RSL, two people had bet me ten dollars I couldn't eat four hamburgers in less than ten minutes and they ran away just as I stuffed the last one in), I decided to hire the boat called *Happy* to give myself a lift.

For a while it worked. I sat at the tiller dressed in a sombrero I'd found and I felt good. In fact, when my three hours were up I thought to myself, no, bugger it, I'll keep *Happy* a bit longer. I'm an only child, I'll do as I please. Sadly, old captain Sandy didn't realise he'd drifted over some oyster leases. My confidence was shattered by two gunshots and a voice yelling at me through a megaphone, telling me if I didn't move off I was a dead man.

Keeping *Happy* longer than I should have proved quite costly for me in the end. With the late fee for the boat and an on-the-spot trespassing fine, I was down about $300. I should have picked *Sleepy*. I could've had *Sleepy* for eight hours at the same price as *Happy* was for three hours. I hated *Happy*.

12

There's a theory that if you drive an automatic car then you're not really driving. I can't drive a manual myself. I learnt to drive in a Gemini TC automatic, so the automatic is all I know. However, I look like I drive a manual because I pretend to drive one even though I have an automatic.

Whenever you plant your foot in a poorly tuned automatic the gears change with such ferocity a wig can be flicked off your head due to the sudden increases in speed–G forces similar to those experienced by astronauts. However, it's because some of the older automatics are jerky that it's easier to pretend they're manuals.

As I take off from lights I touch the T-Bar, rotate my shoulder like I'm operating a manual gearstick, slow down and speed up for authenticity, then let the car do the rest. Sometimes I even pretend I have no synchro in first. To make that convincing, of course I have to stop dead and mime changing into first. This can shock other drivers, but if they hit you from behind, remember they're in the wrong. No amount of punching can change that.

PS Make sure you take any reference to automatic off the outside of your vehicle.

13 When you're attractive it's hard to concentrate

I was at swimming training doing laps. This particular day the coach had chastised me twice for being sluggish. She said if I didn't pick it up I'd have to stay back. I told her the water was like warm milk and it was making me feel lethargic. The real reason was I had an erection and it was acting like an anchor. The reason I had the erection was I was flirting with a woman who was walking along the side of the pool as I was swimming up and down it. Every time I took a breath I saw her looking at me. Breath, look, breath, look. It was like an affair under strobe lighting. This went on for quite a few laps too. The combination of the swimming rhythm and an air bubble that moved about like a blister under her wet Speedos was arousing me.

It wasn't until three of her friends dived in front of me and said, 'We know someone who likes you, but we don't know why cos you're a dog' that things changed. Even though that hurt me it did me a favour because my erection disappeared and my lap times improved, so I didn't have to stay back and do more training.

If I'd been attractive I would have had to stay back.

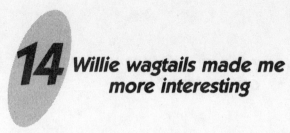

14 Willie wagtails made me more interesting

I do a few things quite well but I don't have one outstanding skill, so sometimes I appear a little flat. This was obvious when I had a crush on Nerida, a strong woman who worked in a jewellery shop. No matter what I did to attract her attention, I made no impression on her.

I tried the usual stuff–pouting to make my lips look more sexy, wetting my eyebrows so they had a crisp line, keeping my arms folded–so my fists pushed my biceps out–but I just looked like everyone else. In fact the only action I got was from two mature Willie wagtails who had some chicks in a nest in the awning above Nerida's shop. I think they saw my full lips, folded arms and crisp eyebrows as a threat and they attacked me. I must have looked very odd trying to avoid those little cantankerous birds as they swooped all about me making their aggressive clicking sound. However, I moved in such an unselfconscious way I suddenly looked original and interesting and that made Nerida look up and take an interest in me. One thing led to another and I asked her out next January.

That's when the Willie wagtails should have their next lot of chicks.

15 A long fringe can get you out of trouble

Whenever we'd had a roast I'd get up after my parents had gone to bed and soak some bread and butter in any leftover gravy I could find. In my haste to get the gravy in my mouth the pan would sometimes move about, like a puppy whose food bowl was on wet lino, and my parents would come out to see what the noise was. I found that if I pulled my hair over my eyes it was like the incident had never occurred. If I couldn't see them then they couldn't see me either. I was totally invisible.

I have a long wavy fringe and when I pull it over my eyes I not only feel mysterious, but I feel as if I'm lying on my stomach staring through a thick crop of lantana and no one can see me. I have naturally thick hair and because I wash it every day I also get a lot of product build-up. Therefore, when I pull my fringe down over my eyes it blocks out the light so effectively that I could almost grow moss on my forehead.

You may look odd tugging at your fringe every time you don't want to be seen, but it does create a natural place for you to hide. You'll never get asked to lift heavy things, do surveys, or get picked to do potentially humiliating things. You'll also look arty and troubled, which adds depth to a person who is easily spooked.

16 *Join an unspoken moment club*

An unspoken moment club is formed when a group of people experience something embarrassing together and don't talk about it again until they're together again. I'm in two unspoken moment clubs. One formed when I saw Kerry Gumley and his neighbour Sofia naked in his garage taking turns to urinate in front of each other. The other one was created when Craig Melvee and I saw Jason Hall in the bath with his mother. Their house was being renovated at the time and you could see right into a few rooms. It was exhilarating to watch Mrs Hall gently bathe her teenage son with a flannel, wrap him in a towel and then carry him into the bedroom, but it was embarrassing to explain it to others who weren't there. So Craig, myself and the Halls formed an unspoken moment club. Sometimes at weddings, twenty-firsts, Year 12 formals or funerals, when all the original participants are present, these clubs meet again.

The people in these clubs seem special to me as they remember their unspoken moments together. The more unspoken moment clubs you're in, the more popular you look. Never do humiliating things alone or you'll be lonely at social functions.

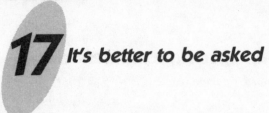

17 *It's better to be asked*

People say things happen to people who make them happen. I think it's better to be asked. When you're asked to join a group or a conversation, somebody wants you to be there, and that somebody has an interest in seeing you succeed too because their judgment is on the line as well.

When you force your way in you have to bump people out of the way and immediately you've got enemies. I hate to be hated. It makes me try too hard to please, and being a crawler is exhausting.

Nevertheless, you need to put yourself in a position to be asked. Stay close to conversations and keep your lips moving, so you're ready to join in at any time. Keep your head pointing up too, so your eyelids look heavier and you appear more relaxed and less desperate. Have three funny lines ready to go, because laughter covers any lack of charisma. We also look more relaxed when our hands are occupied. I'll even hold a chair if I have to, anything to avoid looking awkward. No one will ask you to join in if they think you look awkward or suss.

18 Datsun Homer Van

We'd draw Datsun Homer vans in our class at school.
We'd draw them with a ruler and colour them in so cool.
We would join our tables, a ruler for the gears,
Greenie and I drove up the coast in our Homer van for
years.
In maths or history, tech drawing or exams,
You could hear the hum of our Datsun Homer van.
We'd drive to the Bluepools to Crescent or to Byron,
We'd keep driving till we heard that end of lesson siren.

My dream was the same as Greenie's, his was just like
Dave's.
There were quite a few of us who dug those detailed Datsun
raves.

We used to draw our surfboards in our class at school.
We'd draw them with a ruler and colour them in so cool.
I would make the sounds for Greenie's bottom turns,
He would yelp when I made that water burn.
We'd put our paper boards onto our paper vans,
Take off down the paper roads to get a paper tan.
Taree, Kempsey, Grassy, Coffs, Lennox, Byron,
We'd keep driving till we heard that end of lesson siren.

TWO OF
GREENIE'S IMPRESSIVE
DATSUN HOMER VAN
DRAWINGS. (YEAR 8)

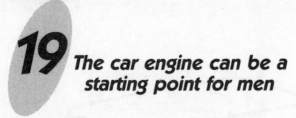

19 The car engine can be a starting point for men

It's amazing how your confidence can go at a garage. It can be as simple as mispronouncing an automobile part, but it can leave a scar that leads to chronic uneasiness whenever you're at a garage, or an automobile literate person's house. My solution–practise sounding knowledgeable on an NRMA person. On an isolated roadside there are no 'mates' for them to give mocking glances to. Not like at a garage, where there can be as many as five men waiting for a man with soft hands to drop a clanger.

Break something on your car so it's an authentic call for help and learn to say a few things like, 'I've got a canary under the hood', so you can kick-start a conversation without sounding like you're a novice. The NRMA person will have more confidence in opening up to you if they feel like you know something to begin with.

It may take five or six visits from an NRMA patrol, but the confidence you gain on an isolated roadside can then be used on established garage mechanics. Remember, if you and another man are experiencing social uneasiness just flip the bonnet up on the closest car and stare at the engine. You'll be surprised how rapidly the conversation will flow.

20 *Jealousy makes you more romantic*

Sometimes in a long-term relationship the romance fades. You don't fall out of love, but you don't try as hard as you once did to make your partner feel loved, such as leaving love notes about, giving surprise gifts, or as in my case, making French toast on Sunday mornings and serving it with the front of my dressing-gown open and nothing on underneath.

Romance is a combination of lust, anxiety, infatuation, fear of loss, the need to be the same and a desire to be touched. It's like a plane with five engines and like all things that fly parts of it break down. The good thing about romance is it can lose several of its engines and still manage to keep flying. That's what I found during my six weeks with Virginia. One by one the engines went out and the romance lost altitude, but it didn't crash. It just landed in a far away place and rusted in a disused hanger. And what was the one thing that kept us flying so we could land safely? Jealousy. When I saw Virginia talking with other men, I got jealous and the fear of losing her made me more romantic.

Encourage your partner to see other people. I guarantee you'll be much more romantic. I was very attentive during those last days with Virginia.

21 If you weep once a week you avoid being bitter

In life there are many disappointments, such as having a pencil case you've just made trashed by the woodwork teacher in front of the class as an example of wood wasting, failing your HSC three times, a fear of commitment that stops you from saying I love you–the list goes on and on. Disappointment is one of our most prevalent natural resources, along with coal, iron ore, wool and tourism.

Disappointment, unfortunately, has very little long-term use. Iron ore is turned into steel, bauxite into aluminium, tourism into jobs, wool into jumpers, but disappointment just turns into bitterness and that can only be used in the arts, or sport, or by people who have just broken up a relationship. There's not a lot of call for bitterness as an export product either.

Disappointment is stored in little tanks behind the eyes, and when they're full they're emptied in the form of a little cry. If they're not emptied, if you try and hide your disappointment, there's often an emotional explosion somewhere down the track. That's why, each week, I have a little cry just to empty the tanks. Even if I don't feel sad it's still good to flush. I'm always disappointed, but I'm not bitter.

Sometimes I have to hit my nose with a ruler to make my eyes water, but that leaves a bruise and I look tougher, which helps cover the fact I cry a lot.

Nerve Hold Someone grabs the muscle that connects the shoulder to the neck between the index, middle finger and the thumb and squeezes it. It has the element of surprise because you can creep up from behind someone and execute it. It can be held for a long time too, and because it's quite painful it's perfect for getting money, tickets to bands and so on from people. It has no lasting physical effects.

Dead Leg A person comes up beside you and knees you in the thigh. It too has an element of surprise. You can be talking with someone, suddenly they knee you in the thigh and temporarily you lose all power in that particular limb. It's useful for making people spill things. It does have some lasting side effects though, such as bruising.

23 *When you overstretch yourself, don't lose sight of the truth*

My very first Gemini had a cassette player, but in order to make more impact I extended the speaker cables so I could park a long way away from the action and still have the speakers right there next to me. If there was an impromptu function in a park or a beer garden, people would often say 'Oh why not get Sandy to come along and then we can have some music!'

At the beach one day everything was perfect. My car was about 100 metres away but both my speakers were right beside me on the sand, playing among other things 'Sexual Healing' by Marvin Gaye. It was wonderful.

Everybody was drinking and dancing to my choice of music. It almost felt like my party. However, as my car was out of sight with the keys in the ignition to power up the cassette player, somebody took the opportunity to steal it. All I saw, as my car sped off down the street, were my two Philips speakers being dragged behind the Gemini like two amateur water skiers. I should have parked the car somewhere I could see it.

If you overstretch yourself don't lose sight of where you're coming from, otherwise you're vulnerable. And when you're vulnerable you can lose face very easily.

24

"I'd like to thank everyone for coming and suck more piss"!/

25

What Mr Gumley was saying about the front gates actually happened to him. It took my father and Mr Gumley over an hour to get his front gates off his bumper bar.

26 I Am My Dad

I know a place out by the island where the channel meets the sandbar.
It's where my grandpa took my dad to fish for whiting or for flounder there.
You'd get up early before sunrise, check the papers for the tides.
You'd get all the rowlocks, get all the oars, get Mr Price 'cause he's a nice guy.
Then I stop and I stare at the things that are there and imagine my dad as a boy.
A hat with a bike, a white singlet and a 1926 smile.
I am my dad as I wonder through the older designs in some of your old style suburbs.

I know a way into the showground through a hole in the grandstand.
It's where my grandpa took my dad to watch the cricket and football finals there.
You get up early before sunrise, check the papers for train times.
Get on the good gear, you shine your shoes, get Mr Price 'cause he's too good to lose.

Then I stop an arm wrestle with Great Grandad in a close thirties family way.
I wish I could love my dad as much as I love his photograph.
I love to go to public bars and feel the architecture,
Then I can know what my dad was like when he was a teenager.

I Am My Dad. Intro - CHORUS STRUCTURE.

VERSE: I know a place out by the island where the channel

meets the sand-bar it's where my grand-pa took my dad

to fish for whit-ing and for floun-der there— You'd

get up ear-ly be-fore sun rise check the pa-pers

for the tides you'd get all the roll-icks get all the oars

get Mis-ter Price 'cause he's a nice guy-------- Then I

stop and I stare at the things that are there and im-a-gine my dad as a

boy a hat with a bike a white sing-let and a nineteen twenty

smile---CHORUS: I am my Dad as I won-der through the

old-er de-signs in some of your old style suburbs Mios.(I)

love to go to the pub-lic bar and feel the arch-i-

-tec-ture Then I will know what my

Dad was like when he was a teen---- a - ger

I am my Dad as I won - der through the

old - er de - signs in some of your old style sub-urbs

27 *Food can help with responsibility*

The night before I was to lead a group on a bushwalk at the 'find the angel in yourself' theatre workshop, I was restless. What if someone got lost or had an accident? What if someone couldn't find their inner angel by Sunday and their parents wanted their money back?

I'd felt this similar uneasiness before when I was in a car with a friend and we were hopelessly lost. My friend stopped at a garage and sent me in to ask the manager for some directions. Instead of returning with a map, or instructions on how to get where we were going, I bought a pie and instantly everything went calm. As I ground the buttery crust into a fine paste, the fear of being responsible for getting us to our appointment on time completely subsided.

With this in mind I got up and put a packet of milk arrowroot biscuits in my knapsack. If the responsibility became too great during the bushwalk tomorrow, I could eat the biscuits and it would feel like I was surrounded by my family and one of them would make everything right for me.

I slept soundly that night, so soundly I slept in and missed the bushwalk altogether. I had a free morning without any responsibility.

28

MR. BUMBLE BEE (as sung by Nigel)

Mr. Bumble Bee
I'm tired and I want to go
to sleep.

Mr. Bumble Bee
my petal is heavy with
pollen don't you see
Mr. Bumble Bee.

29

The only time I tried this method of shoplifting I finished my milkshake too early and you could see the sunglasses through my container.

30 Sky workers have confidence

A sky worker is someone who looks at your forehead when they talk to you. The reason–people feel less inhibited if they don't make eye contact. This was the case when I was a barman at a reception centre. It was an older crowd, equal parts unwanted men unwanted women. The highlight of the night was when some of the patrons took turns at acting out role reversals. In one situation a woman was fitted with an apron that had a large erect penis sewn on the front while the man had an apron with a felt vagina embroidered on it. They were both blindfolded and they had to find each other using only the genitals sewn on their respective aprons. I remember thinking I could never do that. I said as much to one of the men when he was at the bar. 'Aren't you embarrassed doing that sort of thing in public?' I said. 'Not with a blindfold,' he replied. Then it suddenly dawned on me why my Aunty Coral could reveal her private fantasy life so easily. She looked at my forehead when she told me about it. She was a sky worker. If she couldn't see my cynical facial expressions her spirit was never dampened. She was wearing an imaginary blindfold.

Even though I regularly missed the bar when I put the beers down I was more talkative and received more tips that night when I looked at the patrons' foreheads rather than directly into their eyes.

31 *Having a well-shaped bottom is not always an advantage*

A well-shaped bottom, or two bulbous resonators that fill out a pair of tight jeans, is very important to some people. I have no bottom myself, so naturally I don't consider it that important. If I were to lie down on my side you could almost draw a straight line from my back to the top of my thighs. The only reason you couldn't make a straight line would be if the pencil caught in the wiry hair at the base of my spine.

The Gumleys had an older son Mal, who had a set of perfectly formed resonators, or so Virginia once said. However, it was his resonators that lost him quite a few friends in our street.

For a while everyone was intrigued by this car horn that would honk wildly for 50 seconds every second night up near the park. Slowly at first, then very fast. The culprit, according to Mr Fewings*–who knew everything that happened in the street–was Mal's buttocks. Apparently Mal and his girlfriend Peta were being intimate in his car and because his passenger seat was stuck they had to use the driver's seat. Even with the seat fully reclined, Mal's well-formed buttocks still honked the horn with every thrust. I'd have been very quiet myself, not only because I didn't have a partner, but my buttocks would never have reached the horn.

---

* *Sandman's Advice to the Unpopular, page 53*

Unpopular folk often lose the luxury of physical contact. Here's a list of how and where to touch or be touched without legal problems.

1 The hairdressers. If you have thick wavy hair you can experience two hours of touching for around $30.

2 Having someone fix your tie – this has the added bonus of eye contact.

3 Holding money away from the shop vendor, so they have to reach over the counter to grab it.

4 Going for the pedestrian button on traffic lights at the same time as another person.

5 Rainbow markets are full of touchy feely types. You can get a hug from a woman who's wearing old Spanish wine bags just because you've got a sad face.

6 Taking part in an audience participation routine. Buskers often work swiftly, otherwise they lose their audience. They often have to push their volunteers about to get them into position.

7 A good shower can feel like a firm hand.

8 A warm seat. The moment someone gets up from a seat on a bus or train, sit in the same spot and absorb their warmth. Don't close your eyes though, because it may look like you've just farted.

9 Look for a group of three people waiting for a cab. Ask if you can share, and if so, hop in the middle of the back seat and pray you get a reckless driver, so you get tossed from side to side, causing you to fall on the two window seat passengers. Hopefully they're going to the airport and it's easy to get a cab back into town.

33 Make people love you more by using the Conglomerate Rock Technique

People are generally attracted to themselves, therefore it's fair to say if you can adopt other people's characteristics and incorporate them into your own personality, they should find you more interesting. This is the essence of the Conglomerate Rock Technique—an ability to cover your personality with bits and pieces from other people's personalities.

If I'm talking to an academic I'll use more adjectives, make an opening statement backed up by four solid points to mimic the structure of an exam paper, or gesture with my hands more as if I'm speaking at a conference. If I'm with yobbos I'll pretend I've got a hangover, push my pants a little lower and laugh like Ernie Sigley. Be careful with self-loathers. If you try to copy them they may take an instant dislike to you.

The Conglomerate Rock Technique is perfect for people who haven't found themselves yet. It's much easier to cover an ill-formed personality with other people's traits than it is to cover a well-rounded one. There's also less to hide. Be everything to someone by using the Sandman's Conglomerate Rock Technique. People will like you more and no one will ever know, because they'll be too busy loving themselves to notice.

34 *Attention Seeking Device Demonstration*

The Pterodactyl is an authentic re-creation of the prehistoric bird. It's basically a screeching sound, and to be honest, it sounds more like a seagull. Don't do it too often either, because it feels like you're coughing up fish hooks. It is perfect for when you first meet people, when you walk into a room full of strangers, or in a job interview situation. For example, the Mock Job Interview Situation.
(Characters: the Manager, You.)

MANAGER: *Hello (insert your name). Come in.*

YOU: *Thank you.*

MANAGER: *So you're here about the metallurgist's position?*

YOU: *Yes, I am.*

MANAGER: *I'll just have a look through your references and credentials. (look through papers) Oh, I see you've failed the HSC three times.*

YOU: *Cawwww! Cawwww! Cawwww!*

The manager will forget about those poor HSC results straightaway.

35 Use the Danska Creme Effect to achieve a multi-layered personality

Take two sheets of paper and write the same message on both pieces. Leave one piece exactly how it is, but fold the other one as many times as you can until it's a tiny square. Give both bits of paper to a second person. Which piece of paper do you think they'll be interested in ? Answer? The folded piece. Both notes are made from the same stuff, have the same message, but one looks more intriguing simply because it needs to be unfolded in order to be understood.

If you want to look substantial then apply the same principle, or as I call it, the Danska Creme Effect–layer upon layer upon layer–to your personality. That is, hide the obvious parts of your personality under a series of defence mechanisms (folds).

There are two drawbacks with the Danska Creme Effect: if you're impatient you may find that you fold yourself unevenly, thus creating a personality that looks more like a piece of rubbish, and if someone does unfold you, there'll be creases or emotional scars, and these can be hard to get rid of.

A word of warning also to the person who is doing the unfolding. A personality is like a pizza box–it's very hard to close once it's been opened.

36 Anticipation is more charismatic than achievement

Several Christmases ago our guests warmed to me, not because I was funny as I struggled with the wrapping paper on a Christmas present, but they were touched as I shivered in anticipation of what was inside the wrapping paper. However, when I finally unwrapped the present and it turned out to be a Bond's khaki T-shirt I was very angry because it wasn't what I wanted, and I was instantly less likeable. I lost that extra dimension that anticipation gives you. The anticipation gave me a charisma, but when the present was revealed I was morose and dull.

Now when I want to look more charismatic I try not to achieve anything or touch anything. By almost touching something your body and your emotions are full of anticipation. For instance, I'll never actually sit on a chair. I hover 2 millimetres above it. It's tough on my thighs, but because of that extra tension people are drawn to me. They wonder, 'When on earth is he going to sit down?' In other words, Anticipation=Attention. You generate so much charisma hovering above furniture that you could power a small log cabin. Imagine a marriage where you almost tell the truth, or a style of lovemaking where partners never touch. The possibilities are endless.

37 *When you're isolated you can look pathetic*

As part of a group you can change things through weight of numbers. One wrong turn, such as you stopping to tie a shoelace or your friends going home earlier than you from a party, and suddenly you're isolated and vulnerable. Like a marathon runner who loses touch with the leading pack, or a back-up singer whose voice is isolated during a recording session, you can look and sound pathetic.

When I was with Maureen, Nils, Coconut and Raymond in the car park of a Pizza Hut and we verbally attacked some people in a panel van for littering, we felt very strong. However, when I chased one of their discarded serviettes in the sea breeze it caused me to get separated from my party. When I held their greasy serviette in the air I suddenly realised I was not a champion for the environment, but an isolated and rather frightened antelope about to be attacked by some guys with their hair long at the back.

I don't know if you've tried running after eating an anchovy and olive pizza, but it tends to get isolated in your throat. It's very hard to run effectively with a wad of slightly chewed and very salty pizza in your throat.

39 Where to stand when a raft is going down

An idea is like a raft. On this raft there are often several people, but only one person has their hands on the wheel, steering the ship, so to speak, and that's the captain of the idea. If you're vulnerable, frail, or blush easily, it's important that you're not this person. The captain of the idea may give the orders and get all the glory, but they're also the person who goes down with the raft when the idea turns sour. That's why, if I'm ever a part of an idea, project, or ensemble, I stand two back from the captain, just behind the first backslapper, just in front of the fringe dweller (a friend of the captain who gets lost at sea as the idea develops). When you're two back from the captain you're still on the ship, but you don't have any of the responsibility. You can jump off at the first sign of trouble and no one will know. The captain and the backslapper sink without a trace, whereas you're blameless and free to catch another idea before it sails. If you're unpopular it's best to be towards the back of the raft.

40 *Secrets give you power*

If you're asked to keep a secret consider yourself to be a popular person. People who know things about others are always in demand. For example, I was the first to know Hugh Bonnifaces's mother found a finger in a jam jar at the school canteen, or that it was a guy called Brainiac who did the poo in Brother Placidus's milk bottle and put the top back on it. These were good days. People constantly coming up to me asking for information about things only I knew about.

BROTHER PLACIDUS

Somewhere along the line I also picked up a reputation as a rubber lips–a person who can't keep a secret–and suddenly I was off the heat. To counter this I started to make up my own secrets. I capitalised on a report about a missing plane. I said a national security organisation had sabotaged the plane to justify its existence. I added that the aircraft was carrying mustard gas from a chemical weapons storage depot in Townsville and it was crashed on purpose into a dam near Sydney.

Not long after I started spreading this rumour my neighbour Kerry, who looks like me, was severely beaten by three people wearing balaclavas. Be careful, secrets provide power, but they can also be dangerous. On the other hand, complete ignorance was no help to my neighbour Kerry.

41 *Whether or not you lock your car door can affect the way you're perceived socially*

Let's say you need to impress a bohemian type of person. To do this effectively you'll need to look as if you're a free thinker. No matter what lengths you go to to present this image, you can blow it by doing the wrong thing with a passenger door lock. When you get out of a bohemian's car, never lock the door. This gesture will give them the impression you always do as you please. I suggest you even embellish your position by not being ready when your lift arrives. Come to the front door dripping wet with a towel wrapped round your waist and yell out, 'I'm going to program the video first, I won't be a minute'. In other words, make them wait. This is classic, non-locking the passenger door behaviour.

On the other hand, with 'straighty one eighties' always lock your door and return the window right up to the top. This type of person responds to considerate and conformist behaviour. As the straighty one eighty parent puts the car away for the night, I assure you they will take note of your gesture. 'Look Nancy, he or she locked the door and returned the window to its original position.' A positive impression has been made and you're ready to blend in for personal gain.

When you've got little to offer in life, it's the little things that count.

42 Sometimes you can get drunk from too much attention and sometimes it doesn't smell that nice either

The first time I was drunk on attention was when Aunty Coral asked me to show a guest my lovely long eyelashes. Even though my eyes were shut I could smell their full attention and it was intoxicating. So much so it made me do a sexy dance, which was rather unsettling for a six-year-old.

Years later at my eighteenth birthday a few of us were sitting in a car chewing the sediment stuck on the bottom of someone's father's home brew. We were quite drunk. Since I was 18 I was nominated to go and get more beer. As I entered the bar I stumbled on the stairs. I closed my eyes to regain my balance and when I did two things happened. I heard the words 'Go Sandy, go' and I smelt the intoxicating sensation of everyone's full attention. Its spirit entered me like a flock of startled starlings.

When I opened my eyes all I could see in front of me was the parquetry dance floor lapping the carpet area as if it was a tropical lagoon. So I ran towards it and swallow-dived into it, my nose making a loud snapping sound as it connected with the floor. Despite this inconvenience I swam across the slippery tiles, tumble turned and returned doing the back-stroke. I was so drunk on attention I felt no pain. Later at Casualty I realised I was just drunk and that when your nose is broken attention doesn't smell that nice.

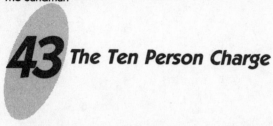

43 The Ten Person Charge

A few years ago, before they introduced bouncers who were trained in the martial arts, there was a very effective way of getting into venues, called the Ten Person Charge. We'd assemble outside a venue and wait until we had at least ten people dressed in a similar style. Not hard when you're a teenager. Then, on a prearranged signal, we'd all pull our shirts over our heads and charge past the door person en masse. Once inside we'd simply pull our shirts down and then act normal. No one saw your face, so it was impossible for anyone to identify you. On average eight people got through and two got caught. The two who got caught were the ones dressed a little bit differently. It was a type of natural style enforcement–only the similar survived.

I did the Ten Person Charge and I'm happy to report I was one of the eight who got in, but because I had on a rather tight blue Midford shirt with the top button done up, the collar got stuck across my eyebrows and I couldn't see where I was going. I ran straight into a table full of drinks and then had to buy all those people fresh beverages. I was inside the club for a minute and I was already down 22 bucks. I also stood out because I was the only one with a shirt over my head.

I'm sorry to say that the introduction of the revolving door at many clubs has meant the end of the Ten Person Charge as an effective social weapon.

44

To use Spud's <u>actual</u> words:

Sandy could get his board and piss off...

(I didn't like the piss off bit)

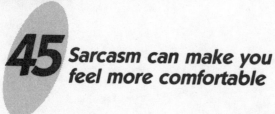

45 Sarcasm can make you feel more comfortable

Sometimes the most difficult thing to do in a new social scene is look comfortable. When I moved cities a few years back I joined an arty crowd, and to be honest I felt very uncomfortable. Postmodern this, deconstruction that, etcetera. That was until I discovered sarcasm.

When someone is being sarcastic it's a sure sign they're comfortable in their surroundings. Sarcasm says to people 'I'm confident, I'm strong, I'm better than you'. Confidence creates comfortableness, and when you're comfortable you look as if you belong. The beauty of sarcasm is it's quite a cold thing too. Using it doesn't drain you emotionally like crawling does. Sarcasm is low key. Do be careful not to overuse it though. Too much sarcasm can make you look as if you're covering a weakness, and vulnerability is the doorway to humiliation.

The disadvantage with using sarcasm as a social tool is you do offend people easily. Only target one person per social scene and you won't make too many enemies on your journey towards comfortableness.

46

# 47 *Beware of human pamphlets*

A human pamphlet is someone who obtains knowledge not from personal experience but from books, magazines, CD covers and so on. When they relay that information to you it tends to be dry and boring–rather like reading a pamphlet.

At school when a teacher gives you a handout, sometimes it won't grab you. Why? It's probably been copied from another book, that's why. It's like telling someone to iron their underpants because they have to. If you personalise the command–for example, 'I personally find the warmth of just ironed cotton on the smooth skin between my legs quite pleasant'–then suddenly that command is made to seem more interesting. Whenever someone relays information through personal experience it adds interest. You can hold a listener better if you add personal revelations.

To help you recognise the human pamphlet here's some of their favourite topics of conversation–tax, obscure information about bands, building materials, sport, cars–for example, how to fix a spongy brake pedal in the TD series of Gemini. By the way, a spongy brake pedal is most likely caused by air in the hydraulic system. Damn! I'm a bloody pamphlet.

48 The $3 Escape Technique

Making a natural break from a boring conversation, or escaping from people who want you to lift a heavy box, can be a difficult thing to do without offending them. Have you ever listened to someone talk about Musica Viva for 20 minutes? Your legs are aching and all you want to do is sit down, but because the person talking is important to you it's hard to break away. That's why I always have $3 worth of loose change loosely rolled in a handkerchief in my pocket. When you can listen no more, simply reach into your pocket, pull out the hanky and the loose coins go everywhere. You say 'Oh, there goes my money'. A natural and legitimate escape has been created. The cost—a mere $3. I suggest a mixture of 10 cent, 20 cent and 50 cent coins, so there's lots of noise. A combination of a $2 and $1 coin won't make a big enough distraction, and the more coins you have the longer it takes to find them, so there's more emotional distance created between you and the people you're escaping from.

Make sure the money in your hanky is not your bus fare home, because if you can't find the coins you may have to go back and ask the people you escaped from for money.

49 The further you are from your subject matter, the easier it is to tell the truth about it

When I was with Virginia I found it hard to be truthful. I felt fine as I drove to pick her up and after I'd dropped her off, but the moment she sat in the passenger seat of my car it was always silence punctuated by nervous coughing, half truths and platitudes. When we were physically close we were emotionally distant.

All this changed when I was heading back to Sydney from Broken Hill. I was held up due to the floods near Nyngan, so I decided to give Virginia a call. It was the best talk we'd ever had. Sensing it was the distance between us that was helping our candidness I turned around and drove west again, stopping at Cobar and Wilcannia to make more calls. The further away I got, the more truthful I became.

Our calls became long rivers of truth. If only Virginia had answered the phone when I called from Broken Hill instead of her father. He was quite severe with me and told me to stop ringing up all the time. I suspect he would have said the same thing to my face because he had a natural distance from others. I guess his method of telling the truth was more practical too. The costs sure do add up with all that travelling.

50 By staying out of reach, Don ensured that he was always a talking point

I didn't know anyone in my area that didn't want to know more about Don, but no one ever got close enough to find out anything about him. When everyone else was out socialising, he'd sit up in the tree in front of the library and read poetry. On Saturday nights when couples went to the movies, he'd retrieve papers caught high up on the cliff face at the beach. After midnight he'd take his German shepherd, Dominic, to the local pizza bar and they'd both bark at people getting takeaway.

I went through school intrigued by Don, but not knowing very much about him. I knew he was always the first person across the pedestrian crossing at infants school, but even then he'd run off down the lane lined with mulberry trees and disappear from view. At high school, when he got his licence, he put a straight eight into his car with the money he'd saved from having no social life and he'd drive away from school at a thousand miles an hour. No one could catch up to him to find out where he went because most students only had second-hand V dubs, or they caught the bus.

Recently I was at Manly (a place that smells like little bottles of oysters) and I saw Don singing in a band. At the end of their lacklustre set I went over to make myself known to him again, but by the time I got to the stage area he'd already gone home.

51 An overdependence on your parents is often a contraceptive

Every Sunday morning I'd lie in bed waiting for a sign from the master bedroom that my parents were awake. Perhaps it was the sound of a bedspring, a sigh of resignation, a dry cough, or even a wake-up fart–a trait common to the men in my family. We're traditionally slow starters and the fart acts like a genetic snooze button.

The moment I heard something I'd leap out of my bed and bound into theirs. I'd just lie there, snuggled in between them both, and read a comic, or stare at an ad on the back page of the newspaper for a chipboard submarine that you could order by coupon.

If you could have hovered above our house and looked down, we'd have looked like a sombre postage stamp on a queen-sized envelope waiting to be sent somewhere better–me in the middle and two miserable adults on either side. Miserable because, as I later learned, Sunday morning was their traditional sex time. My morning invasions were perhaps one reason I was an only child. The fact that I was scared of the dark and spent many nights in their bed didn't help either.

52

The Haaatherear is created by making a nasal sounding 'aarrh' noise, then opening your mouth quite wide and shutting it again with a snapping motion. The noise you make should sound like Haaaathereaaarrrr! The haaatherear is a perfect linking device if you're having trouble holding a listener, or if you're trying to buy time in order to think of something clever.

The Lip Trumpet A trumpet sound is made by resting your top row of teeth on your bottom lip. When you make an 'aah' sound your lips vibrate against your teeth and it sounds like a trumpet. I generally play 'When the Saints Go Marching In' or 'Rock Around the Clock' by Bill Hayley.

Peg Leg is a short appraisal of Herman Melville's novel *Moby Dick*. You stick your index finger in your mouth and pop it against the inside of your cheek thus using the mouth like an echo chamber. If you're doing it right it should make a low popping sound. If you tighten your cheek and do the same as before, a higher pitched popping sound is created. When the two popping sounds are made one after the other, it gives the impression someone with a wooden leg is walking across floorboards, or as in the case with *Moby Dick*, Captain Ahab pacing on the quarterdeck.

Skeleton Teeth Make a person sit opposite you and say 'I'm going to create a unique moment but at no time will I touch you'. You get in real close to the person and then, when the moment's right, you furiously pull the loose skin on your cheeks in and out, thus creating the impression your teeth are rattling. If everything goes well you should give the person opposite a surprise and thrill those watching you at the same time. The set-up to skeleton teeth can go on for up to ten minutes.

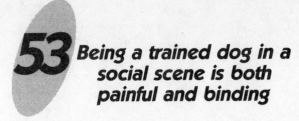

53 Being a trained dog in a social scene is both painful and binding

A trained dog is someone who'll do anything on command to be noticed. At my school Craig Ritter was our trained dog. He'd eat a cockroach for money, or drink muddy water for a packet of chicken-flavoured chips. So whenever we were bored we'd get him to do something. Who'll climb the Kmart flagpole and steal the giant flag? 'Craig will.' Sure enough, up he'd go, barking loudly to cover his fear of heights.

The routine that established him and became his staple was when he'd get people to line up at lunch, then, one by one, ask them to say, 'Batman calling' to him. The moment they said it, he'd lick the closest wall and pick up any empty bottles in his field of vision. He'd repeat this routine over and over, like a dog who never tires of chasing a frisbee. The saddest thing was when he didn't feel like responding. People sometimes got angry and punched him just as if he was a disobedient animal.

A trained dog is always in demand, but by jingo it's a hard way to earn your attention.

54

George Sharko
49 Pleasant Avenue

To whom it may concern,

My name is George Sharko (Nil's father).
We met once when our cat was stuck in
your gum tree. Normally I don't get involved
in this type of affair, but I feel it's my civic
duty to bring to your attention an incident
involving your son. Last Saturday we had
some friends from Egypt visiting which incid-
ently included their children who ranged from
2 yrs to 13 yrs. We were all enjoying the sun,
surf and company of good friends when your
son was involved in one of the most unsettling
exhibitions of public indecency I've ever wit-
nessed. If you haven't heard, he was
running around completely naked on the beach
making a noise like an air-craft engine
and, if that wasn't bad enough, when he
flew past where we were located, he moved
~~✱~~ in a very rude way. Not only
was he a poor ambassador for our country,
it was unsettling for the children who
had to witness his puerile and tasteless
display.

I'm sorry I have to relay this to you by letter, but to do it face to face would make me too angry. We were not the only ones affronted by his act of poor manners. Sandy is no longer welcome at our house.
Yours faithfully,
George Sharko.

55 Rushing makes you feel like an executive

When you rush you feel like an important executive in charge of a large group of people. That's why I cram everything I do into a small part of each day. In my diary, in the space between 8 and 8.30, I write the following: get up, go to toilet, eat breakfast, get dressed, drive to shops, drive back home. I keep my writing very small and hard to read, so at a glance all the items look like they are real appointments. So between 8 and 8.30 I'm often flustered, I miss breakfast, I tend to drive quickly, if someone rings up I have to ring them back and if I have to wait in line at the shops I get agitated, just like a real executive with a busy schedule does.

The only problem with rushing in small bursts is that there is often nothing to do after 9 o'clock. During daylight saving this can be quite harrowing. I find if I put on a floral shirt and some bermuda shorts and pretend I'm on holidays it helps. I also draw out 17 per cent of whatever money I have in the bank and pretend it's a holiday loading. If I can get a stranger's address and send them a postcard this also adds realism as well. Rushing makes me feel executive class.

56 *If you're awkward don't hug anyone because you may get injured*

At a recent function I was shocked to see how many of my acquaintances had scars on their eyebrows or unnatural bumps on their noses. One woman was even holding a fresh cut together with her fingers as we chatted. The reason for this outbreak of peer scarring became obvious during the formal greetings that followed each new guest's arrival. As we welcomed each other we were so damn tense that when we hugged we accidentally head-butted each other. No one knew where to place their head, let alone their lips.

If you have to embrace someone and you find hugging uncomfortable, keep your head down and lead with your forehead. If you do clash heads at least you hit with the hard part of your skull instead of your eyebrows or nose.

If you're introduced to someone with fresh scars over both eyes and they have arms that when they move resemble two teak chair legs, don't hug them just in case they're awkward.

Epilogue

My favourite thing is seeing someone miss out on something they desperately want, so if this book doesn't live up to your expectations at least you know I'll be happy.

The end.